S0-CFX-166

NIKKI REED had jazzed up her act, striving to become the Bayou's most popular performer. Then Victor swept into her life, determined to make her a "lady." She was flattered by his attention but suspicious of his motives. What did he *really* want?

VICTOR NEWMAN thrived on power. Having achieved success in the business world, he now sought to control individual lives—starting with Nikki Reed.

GREG FOSTER had tried to rid his mind of Gwen, the lovely redhead who had stolen his heart then suddenly disappeared. So why did he still see her face in every crowd . . . hear her voice in every sound?

Erika Bryant is the pseudonym for a husband and wife writing team whose books range from Regencies to contemporary romances. Native Midwesterners, they live with their children and pets in a suburb outside Chicago.

From the editor's desk...

Dear Friend,

Captivating . . . exciting . . . heartwarming! These are but a few of the comments we've received from Soaps & Serials readers. We're delighted. Every month the fine writers and editors at Pioneer pool all their resources to bring you brand-new spectacular books.

Based on actual scripts from THE YOUNG AND THE RESTLESS, each novel is written with you in mind. Soaps & Serials take you back to the very beginning of the show, revealing the innocent and infamous pasts of your favorite characters, recreating cherished moments from your favorite episodes. And though each book is a complete, satisfying read, our sensational cliffhanger ending is just a hint of the drama that will unfold in next month's Soaps & Serials book.

We receive numerous requests for previous volumes of Soaps & Serials. If you are also curious about how it all began—or if you want to complete your collection—please see the order form inserted in this book.

For Soaps & Serials,

Rosalind Noonan

Rosalind Noonan
Editor-in-Chief
Pioneer Communications Network, Inc.

The Young and the Restless

14

FREE SPIRIT

William J. Bell and Lee Phillip Bell, Co-Creators, Executive Producers, and Head Writers

PIONEER COMMUNICATIONS NETWORK, INC.

Free Spirit

THE YOUNG AND THE RESTLESS paperback novels are published and distributed by Pioneer Communications Network, Inc.

ISBN: 1-55726-253-5

Printed in Canada

10 9 8 7 6 5 4 3 2 1

Between the Lines

Based on the popular Pygmalion theme, Victor and Nikki were one of daytime's most unlikely couples. Victor was rich and dashing, a true gentleman. Nikki, on the other hand, was anything but a cultured lady. As a stripper in a local night club, she had earned quite a reputation in Genoa City. Yet they were drawn together by a force far more powerful than their vast differences. This book explores the beginnings of their stormy love affair.

When Victor and Nikki became a hot item in Genoa City circles, viewer mail poured in, and the producers knew they had struck gold. One thing the writers hadn't counted on, however, was the fans' fierce loyalty to Nikki. It seems the audience felt it vital that Nikki not deny her unique personality just to please Victor. The producers listened, and Nikki remained a spunky, colorful character.

Chapter One

Fighting to Forget

"Fool," Victor Newman muttered to his reflection in the mirror above his bar. "You are indeed an old fool."

He reached for a glass and tossed in some ice, the sound echoing through his silent home like pebbles thrown into a dry well. The scotch came next. He poured the amber liquid over the glistening cubes, glanced briefly at the soda and rejected it, then strode into the den and threw himself into his favorite chair. The mahogany-colored leather matched his mood. It was the only dark item in his den, which was paneled in bleached knotty pine and further brightened by an Oriental rug. When he came home, tired and brooding, the leather chair welcomed him like a friendly little island.

He drank deeply of the scotch, reveling in the burning, pain-laden trail it blazed down his throat and into his stomach. Was he a fool or was he just getting old? Or worse yet, was he suffering from a combination of the two maladies?

Victor took another deep drink, but this swallow did not bring a repetition of the satisfying blaze of pain. The first swallow's fire had left his passages benumbed.

He should have brought the wench home. At the very least, he should have stayed and watched her performance. He lifted his glass and took another sip, but grimaced at the taste of ice water. He went to the bar, drowned the sweating cubes in scotch, and returned to his chair.

Even now he could feel the sweat bead on his forehead as he thought of Nikki, her undulatingbody crowding into his mind and senses: long blond hair, much too blond for eyebrows that she obviously didn't pluck, shapely legs with just a hint of muscle to them, and curves that were soft enough to sleep on. Nikki seemed to have been born to live on her back, to feed on the fierce, hot flames of the passion that she lit in men.

Victor let the glass fall from his hand and listlessly watched the remaining liquid paint an amber stain on his Kashan rug. No, he wasn't too old. That wasn't the reason he had denied his natural appetites and turned away from Nikki's bountiful body.

But he was a fool. He was as foolish as any lovesick junior high school student.

Julia was gone. She had taken her grace, her soft natural beauty, and her refinement. She had left him alone with empty arms, an empty house, and an empty soul. Nikki could bounce into his life and surround him with her sensual vitality, but she couldn't fill his emptiness. Only one person could do that, and she was gone. Julia was gone forever. His wife, his love, had left; she had been driven away by his pride and stubbornness.

"Can't that wait until tomorrow?" Chris Foster asked.

Her heart ached as she looked at her brother-in-law. Greg was studiously bent over his desk, papers covering almost the entire scratched surface. The floor of the cubbyhole that was his office was littered with more papers and books. The budget for the Legal Aid Center was small, but while Greg was content to work amid shabby furnishings, he refused to skimp on law books. Although the clients didn't get first-class surroundings, they got first-class legal assistance.

"Greg," Chris prodded when he did not respond, "it's late. You should go home. You can finish that up tomorrow."

"My life doesn't have any tomorrows," Greg said. "And I still have a lot to do today."

Pity, sadness, compassion—all passed through Chris's mind, after weighing heavily on her heart. She knew it wasn't just a heavy work load that was keeping Greg at his desk for such long hours; this obsession with work was merely a diversion, an attempt to ignore his loneliness. Poor Greg. He was young and handsome, a good man with so much to give the right woman. Unfortunately, he hadn't found her yet. He tried so hard, but love just didn't seem to work out for him.

He'd even made a play for Chris, but that had happened a while ago when feelings were strained between her and Snapper. After her marriage righted itself, Greg had once again found himself on the outside looking in. Then he'd fallen hard for Gwen Sherman, but that hadn't worked out either. His subsequent marriage to Nikki Reed had just been a reaction to the heartbreak Gwen had given him. And now that Nikki had left him, he undoubtedly felt that he had nothing and no one.

Chris sat on the edge of his desk and put her hand on his arm, but he ignored her and continued studying the legal brief in front of him.

"You need to get out, young man," Chris told him.

"Yeah, I will." He made some notes in the margin. "I'm going to grab a sandwich later on."

"You know what I mean," Chris said quietly.

He continued working until Chris pulled the papers from under his hands. Greg didn't protest. He simply gave her a resigned, tired look that worried her more than an irritated "Mind your own business" would have.

"You need to get out among other people," Chris said. "Especially female-type people."

"Might I remind you I just went through a divorce?" Greg said. "I'm still in mourning. I'm not ready to associate with 'female-type' people yet."

"You're better off now that your so-called marriage has been canceled."

The muscles around his mouth and eyes tightened, but Greg didn't say anything. He just reached out to take the brief from under her hand.

Chris relinquished her scolding tone. "Greg, let me introduce you to one of my friends."

He tried pulling at the papers, but Chris was leaning all her weight on her hand. Now that she'd started, she wasn't going to let go.

"Greg, please. I want to help you."

"Fine," he replied impatiently. "If you know a woman who wants a free dinner and a few laughs, I have no problems with that."

He gave in so easily that she was suspicious. "Promise?"

"I said it's fine."

Chris stood up and let Greg retrieve his papers. "This Saturday okay?"

He shrugged. "Far be it from me to be the cause of a woman sitting at home on a Saturday night."

Although Chris knew he had acquiesced just to be rid of her, she felt enthusiastic. Maybe it would work out. "I'll find somebody nice," she promised, patting his arm.

Greg just gritted his teeth, saying nothing as he stared at the papers in front of him. When he heard the outer door shut behind Chris, he let go, allowing his body and spirit to sag. There were times when he wished life would just leave him alone, go and find someone else to torment.

He shuffled the papers a bit, trying to make the words catch his interest again, but their power was lost now. His work had been his lifeline since he'd lost Gwen, but even that was starting to weaken. The only thing that drove him some mornings was his clients' needs. He defended people who didn't have the money to buy expensive legal services, but required an attorney's assistance.

The vision of a woman danced above the straight chair in front of his desk. She had a beautiful young face framed by flaming red tresses. *Gwen, my dear sweet Gwen*, he thought. They had been through so much together —findinglove and defeating the powers of evil that had been enslaving her. But after all of that, she'd found a new course for her life, and there had been no room in it for him. He still had trouble believing that she was gone, that she had chosen to dedicate herself to God rather than build a life with him.

Vulnerable and disillusioned, he had been ripe for picking by Nikki Reed. Beautiful, voluptuous, sexy Nikki . . . on second thought, maybe she had been the ripe one. Greg couldn't think of any words to adequately describe that blond bombshell. She exuded such an aura of animal vitality. When she walked into a room, men were burned beyond all redemption. Even truly spiritual men were fired with the flames of passion. Her smile destroyed marriages, dashing the couple's mutual love and respect when she won the husband's infatuation. How could any man resist Nikki's magnetism?

She had desperately needed legal help when she was accused of having murdered her father. Things had looked so bad for her that several lawyers had refused to take the case; Greg had been her last hope.

He'd defended her, and Nikki had been acquitted. Then he'd found himself caught in her spell. He'd seen more and more of her until he finally asked her to marry him. Greg hadn't been sure why she accepted his proposal, but he soon saw that it hadn't been for love. Gratitude? Convenience? Whatever her reason, marriage had meant one thing to him and something entirely different to her. A home and kids weren't in her game plan, and divorce had been inevitable. But still, he had been hurt. Or was his pain caused by the emptiness that now seemed to surround him again? There was no one to keep his mind from wandering back to Gwen, to keep his heart from aching for her.

Greg stood and stacked the papers on his desk haphazardly. Weren't busy fingers supposed to keep the mind busy, too?

Chris was going to find somebody for him

—somebody sweet and gentle and nice, he hoped. Somebody with whom he could have a satisfying relationship. Maybe his heart would never soar again with the joy of unbounded love, but it needed to smile again.

Chapter Two

Bouncing Back

"Joan," Kay Chancellor screamed from her office at Chancellor Industries. "Get in here."

"Yes, Mrs. Chancellor."

Kay stared a moment at the supervisor of her accounts payable section. As always, the mousy little woman, looking even smaller in the expanse of Kay's high-ceilinged office, projected an aura of gray about her: gray hair, pale skin, and dark clothes that looked as if they'd had the life washed out of them long ago. Joan's voice quivered and her hands shook. Kay paused a moment to savor the feeling of power that the woman's fear always gave her.

Then, sighing, Kay forced herself to concentrate on the business at hand. "Don't we always take all discounts available when we pay our bills?"

"Yes, ma'am."

"Well, my dear Mrs. Bransom, I reviewed

15

today's accounts payable register, and I saw no indication of any discounts taken."

"The . . . the discounts are usually given to companies that pay within ten days of receiving the invoice."

"I'm aware of that." Kay had to fight to suppress a smile that wanted to dance on her lips. The little mouse was shaking even more, now that she'd heard the ice in her employer's voice.

"A number of our payments have exceeded the ten-day limit, Mrs. Chancellor." The woman's throat convulsed as she swallowed hard. "In fact, some of them are up to sixty days late."

Kay compressed her lips in a look of annoyance familiar to all employees at Chancellor Industries.

"Mr. Newman has to approve the larger payments," the supervisor hurried to explain. "And he's been so busy lately that—"

Kay waved her hand to silence the woman. "Have the checks been sent out yet?"

"No, ma'am."

"Destroy them," Kay ordered. "Then rerun the payments computer program, and this time demand all available discounts regardless of the age of the invoice."

The woman stood frozen, as if glued to her spot.

"Is there a problem, Mrs. Bransom?"

"I don't think our vendors will like that," she said.

"I don't really care," Kay snapped. She turned her attention to some papers on her desk.

"Mr. Chancellor prided himself on Chancellor Industries having the highest standards of ethics," Joan Bransom said. "He would not have wanted us to take discounts we hadn't earned."

"I'm running a business, Joan, not a Boy Scout camp," Kay snapped. "Furthermore, I don't give a tinker's dam what Mr. Chancellor would or would not have wanted."

The supervisor's chin started quivering at this blasphemy against the sainted Philip Chancellor. Kay found his spotless reputation highly irritating.

"Get out of here and do as I told you," Kay ordered.

After the woman left, Kay leaned back in her chair, tapping her desk with a pencil. The company had been going to pot lately. Damn Victor. He hadn't been staying on top of things. He was still mooning over that ex-wife of his. Kay called Victor's secretary.

"Sue," she said, "is Mr. Newman in his office?"

"Yes, he is, Mrs. Chancellor," the secretary answered, "but he left word that he was not to be disturbed under any circumstances."

"Thank you, Sue. I certainly won't disturb him."

Kay rose from her chair. No, she wasn't going to disturb Victor. She was going to shake

17

him until all the teeth in his head rattled. She moved quickly and purposefully down the hall and stalked past Victor Newman's open-mouthed secretary.

"Sue," Victor said in a tired voice as Kay stepped through the door, "I said I didn't want to be disturbed under—"

"I have no intention of disturbing you," Kay said coolly. "But I plan to throw you out on the seat of your pants if you don't shape up."

He spun his chair around, fighting to control his obvious annoyance while he stared at her. Kay sat down in one of the chairs in front of his desk and put her feet up on the other.

"Do you enjoy the good life, Victor?"

He slowly nodded his head.

"Then you'd better forget about that little parasite who walked out on you."

A dark frown appeared on Victor's face, but Kay only laughed.

"I'll admit that she was a classy lady," Kay went on. "But she was living off you. She wasn't contributing anything of value to this world, and in my book that makes her a parasite."

"She made enormous contributions," Victor said. "She helped entertain people of consequence, and she put Chancellor Industries in a positive light before the community by serving on various charitable and cultural boards."

"Window dressing," Kay snorted. "Go find yourself another pedigreed pet."

Victor looked down at his desk and began playing with a crystal paperweight. "There isn't anyone else like Julia in the world," he murmured.

"The truth of that statement exists only in your mind," Kay said.

He merely shrugged, indicating that he had no desire to argue.

"Victor, Victor," Kay said with sudden gentleness. "The business has been going to hell around here the past few weeks. I can't afford that, and I will not tolerate it."

"I'll take care of things," he snapped and turned his back on her.

Kay was tolerant of a number of things, but inattention wasn't one of them. "If you don't want one of your heavy glass toys buried in your head, I would suggest that you turn around and look at me while I'm talking to you."

Slowly Victor turned to face her.

"Now, listen to me," Kay said, staring hard to hold his attention. "You are not the first person to get yourself enmeshed in an emotional trauma. As a woman, I've gone through the whole range of love roles."

She stretched her lower back, crossed her ankles, and looked into the tent she had formed with her fingers.

"I've been a dutiful daughter, a loving wife, and a doting mother." She collapsed her hands together, interlocking her fingers, and glanced up at Victor. "Each of those roles was very tiring. Emotional entanglements drain a person and give little or nothing in return. And one's basic physical needs usually go unsatisfied."

His eyes wavered and he finally had to look away.

"Now I just concentrate on satisfying my own needs," Kay said with a smile. "I am no longer weighed down with emotional baggage. Consequently, I am more relaxed and I thoroughly enjoy life."

"You may have something there," Victor mumbled.

"I do, Victor. Believe me I do."

She paused to study him. She actually liked Victor a great deal. He had certainly shaped up Chancellor Industries, making it much more profitable than it had ever been, and she wanted to continue that mode of operation. To get the old Victor back, she would have to banish Julia from his mind.

"You have needs," Kay said. "Don't deny them—satisfy them. Find yourself a lush young female body and enjoy yourself."

She could see the uncertainty in his eyes.

"I don't mean some cheap woman, if that's not your style. Pets come in all shapes and styles. Some of them are mutts you find in the city pound and others have long, distinguished pedigrees. The common element is that you can buy whatever you want. All you have to decide is how much you want to pay."

Victor nodded almost imperceptibly. Kay smiled.

"As a bonus," she said, "I am willing to authorize Chancellor Industries to find and house a pet for you."

His eyes flickered as he stared at her.

"I will authorize my agents to look in Chicago, New York, and Europe, if you wish. They will bring the women here, and you can try them out, so to speak."

For the first time Victor laughed. "Kay," he exclaimed, "you're a gem."

"Well?"

"Not right now," he replied. "I already have some of my own irons in the fire."

Kay shrugged and then stood up. "Keep me informed," she said. "I want my president to be happy and satisfied."

"I'm touched."

"Don't be," Kay snorted. "As long as you keep me rich, everything will be fine. If I start getting less rich, it'll be bye-bye, Victor."

His smile turned hard, but it stayed in place. "We understand each other, Kay. We always have."

She nodded and left. As Victor stared at the closed door, his smile remained in place, though it grew cold. Kay was right. There was no sense in mourning a woman as easily replaceable as Julia. What had she done that someone else couldn't be trained to do? It wasn't Julia causing his upset, he realized, but the fact that she had left him, that the choice had not been *his*.

All his life he'd taken control of things, of people and of situations. It was his pride that was hurting, nothing else, and his ego would soon be soothed. Never again would a woman control him—not with her body, not with her tears.

"Why don't you order for both of us?" Barbara Lewis suggested with a cloying smile as she closed the menu.

Greg Foster gritted his teeth. Why should he order? He didn't know what this stranger liked to eat. This whole date was a mistake; he never should have let Chris talk him into it.

"I've never been in a place like this," she said, fingering the white linen tablecloth reverently. "I just wouldn't know what's good."

He glanced at her briefly, trying to force himself into a better mood. After all, it wasn't her fault that she wasn't Gwen, or even Nikki. She was a nice, pretty woman, just what he had claimed he wanted. So why, then, did every word from her mouth irritate him?

"Which would you prefer?" he asked, making an effort to be pleasant. "Beef, fish, or chicken?"

His date shrugged and continued smiling. "It doesn't matter," she replied. "Whatever you're having will be fine. Daddy always said I was easy to please."

Dropping his eyes to the menu, Greg sighed inwardly. Barbara had been a college classmate of his sister-in-law, who had told him again and again how sweet she was. Well, Chris was certainly right about that. The woman was so sugary sweet she almost made him gag.

He forced himself to look at the menu. Maybe he just wasn't being fair. No doubt a nursery school teacher had to be wholesome. And maybe, just maybe, he didn't know how sophisticated women acted. His relationship with Gwen hadn't included many candlelit dinners, not while he was trying to free her from the hold her pimp had on her. And Nikki . . . well, during her trial and after it, she had attracted so much attention that normal dating had been out of the question. But then, Nikki was the type who would always call attention to herself.

Stop lingering on the past, Greg firmly told himself, and got back to the business of ordering dinner. "I'll have the chicken in white wine sauce," he said.

"That sounds good."

"You have a choice of potato and vegetable."

Barbara shrugged.

"How about a twice-baked potato and green beans amandine?"

She nodded, the inane smile never leaving her face.

"I'm going to have blue cheese dressing on my salad," he said. "What would you like?"

23

"I've never had blue cheese. That sounds interesting."

He took a deep breath, let it out slowly, and signaled for the waiter. Barbara didn't want a drink before dinner, so Greg ordered a house wine with their meal. *Give her a chance*, he told himself. Gentle femininity was what he wanted. He had to give her—and himself, too—a chance to relax.

"It must be very satisfying to be able to help so many people," Barbara told him.

Her smile beamed at him and her eyes glistened. Greg had a fleeting impulse to reach for his sunglasses, but pushed it aside. "I never really thought of it that way," he said. "Doctors and nurses help people more than lawyers do."

"No, you really do help people," she insisted. "Poor, desperate people who really need your services. You're not just getting scoundrels off on a technicality."

"I guess you're right." Wasn't that the reason he'd gone into legal aid—to help those who couldn't afford expensive attorneys? Why, then, wouldn't he admit it to her? His mouth felt dry, and Greg wished he had a drink. He looked around, but the waiter was off on the other side of the dining room.

"Which of your cases would you say was the most socially meaningful?"

Greg blinked away from the sincerity shining in her eyes and lowered his head to study the tablecloth. Socially meaningful? He'd sent a

pimp to jail for beating the prostitute who
worked for him. And he'd helped win an
acquittal for a woman who had killed her father
to keep him from raping her. Had he argued
any other socially meaningful cases? Cases that
he could discuss with a small-town girl who
taught four-year-olds how to jump and sing.

Glancing up, he saw the waiter approaching
their table in tuxedoed dignity. "Ah," he said,
letting the welcome relief spill out, "here come
our salads."

Much to Greg's delight, the waiter managed
their meal with smooth efficiency, enabling
him to concentrate on his food, and the pauses
between courses were taken up by refilled wine
goblets and coffee cups. The conversational
requirements were minimal, and Greg was able
to get away with innocuous questions about
Barbara's work and about her college days with
Chris.

"Dessert, sir?"

Greg forced his facial muscles to relax.
Would he have to choose dessert for Barbara?"

"I'd like a dish of vanilla ice cream," Barbara
said.

Greg almost laughed in relief. She could
make a decision. He shook his head in answer
to the waiter's questioning glance.

"I just love vanilla ice cream," she said. "I
could eat it all day. No sauce, no fruit topping,
just plain old vanilla."

Greg nodded.

"I guess I'm just a vanilla kind of person." There was an easy comfort in her voice that he almost envied.

"That's nice," he said.

"Most little girls are," she said, nodding her head for emphasis. "What's your favorite dessert?"

"I'm not much for desserts," he said. "They all taste the same, too sweet."

"I bet you like chocolate," she said. "Little boys like chocolate. They like things with a strong, definite flavor. Little girls tend to like simple things." She frowned momentarily. "Some people say we're bland, but I don't think that's so."

Fortunately, Barbara's dessert arrived just then. As she quietly ate it, Greg figured that she rarely drank, and the wine was causing her tongue to loosen.

He wondered what they should do after dinner. Going to a movie seemed so juvenile, and he really wasn't in the mood to go dancing. It was too much effort trying to keep up a conversation with Barbara; they just didn't seem to be on the same wavelength.

A singer and a comedian were performing at the hotel. Greg had heard that both were conservative and popular with the fried-chicken-and-apple-pie set.

"Would you like to catch the show at the hotel?" he asked.

"Oh, yes," she exclaimed. "Some of the

other teachers at the nursery school went, and they said the acts were real good. Even the comedian was good. He was funny without using profanity."

"Good," Greg said. "Then that's where we'll go." He looked at his watch. "We'd better move along. The first performance is at eight."

He signaled the waiter. He could make a quick drive to the hotel, spend two hours watching the show, and then take Barbara home. He would be home and in bed by eleven.

The nightclub act was unintrusive, and Greg was able to let his mind wander. What kind of women could he love? Gwen . . . Nikki . . . . One made his heart burst with love; the other awakened his passions with a startling fervor. But neither woman had made him feel completely fulfilled.

"He's such a funny man," Barbara said.

Greg nodded and joined in the polite clappingfor the comedian's performance. A tall man in a tux came on stage. "Ladies and gentlemen, we are proud to present to you, fresh from a European tour, Miss—"

How could this singer be fresh after such a tour? Greg wondered. He really didn't care about the answer, and his mind went back to brooding on his problems. Why couldn't he find the kind of love that Snapper and Chris had? Or at least the satisfaction in his work that Chris had?

"She has a beautiful voice," Barbara said.

Greg nodded. Maybe there was something wrong with him. Maybe something deep and dark in his past made him seek out women who would ultimately leave him. Here he was, sitting with a nice girl, counting the minutes until he could be rid of her. Maybe he wasn't normal and should see a psychiatrist. Snapper could probably recommend one.

"Would you folks like another drink?"

Greg regarded the cocktail waitress for a long moment.

"Sir?" she repeated.

He blinked rapidly, as if he were brushing at the cobwebs in his brain.

"If you stay for the second show we have to charge you another minimum." She shrugged, as if the rule embarrased her. "It's Friday night and we get a lot of people on weekends."

"Oh, sure," Greg replied. He cleared his throat and turned to his date. "Ah, I have a busy schedule tomorrow. And it begins early in the morning."

"There are a lot of people in this world who need your legal help," Barbara said sympathetically. "Aren't there?"

"Yeah, I guess so." He turned to the waitress. "I'll take the check now."

Their drive home was quiet. When they reached her apartment, Greg escorted Barbara to the door and planted a light kiss on her cheek.

"You take care of yourself, now," Barbara

said in her best motherly tone. "Let me know how you are."

Greg nodded, gave her a wave, and was quickly gone. Maybe he should become a monk.

"Hit me again."

The bartender paused in his polishing and stared hard at his customer.

"Don't worry," Victor told him. "I'm not driving."

"Hey, no skin off my teeth." The man took his glass, refilled it with scotch, and squirted some soda at the ice cubes bobbing in the amber liquid.

Victor Newman's lips twisted sardonically. The Bayou was some high-class joint. Not only did they give him a repeat in the same glass, but they didn't even bother to give him fresh ice cubes.

The bartender set Victor's drink in front of him and leaned forward, his elbows on the shiny bar. "The boss, though, he tends to get a little tense when a customer wraps himself around a tree. It's a little hard to negotiate those curves on the way into town."

"I imagine so," Victor sneered. "Especially when they're covered with snow."

"Our customers are talented," the bartender said. "They don't even need snow. They can smash up their cars any season of the year."

Victor just grunted. He looked up at the stage in the center of the horseshoe-shaped bar and hoped that the undulating brunette would give it a rest soon. Her obvious boredom was giving the joint all the zing of a funeral parlor.

"It doesn't look like Bambi's raising your temperature," the bartender observed.

Victor grimaced as he set his glass down. "I prefer blondes," he muttered. He hated all brunettes, now that Julia was gone.

"Everybody loves blondes when Nikki's around." The bartender's face was twisted into a look of disdain.

There was something in the man's eyes that bothered him, but Victor couldn't put his finger on it. The last drink, his fourth, was spreading a pink haze all through him, and his mind just wanted to relax.

"You got something against blondes?" Victor's question came out somewhat slurred, but he blamed it on his slightly numb lips.

"Actually," the bartender replied, "I like them all."

The pink haze cleared for an instant. "To each his own, buddy," Victor snarled.

Victor waited, every sense alert, to see what the man's response would be. But both were distracted by the sound of a different and livelier tune from the Bayou's loudspeakers.

"I'd better go get the mop," the bartender sneered. "The old men always start drooling when Nikki shakes it."

Victor stared hard. Nikki wasn't doing anythingexceptional or unusual with her body. Actually it was a standard bump and grind, yet the woman's sensuality covered the bar like a blanket of fog.

What was it that made Nikki so special? She had a well-shaped body, but she could never be a model. Most women would consider her a tad too heavy. Her lips were a little too generous, and her hair was too thick. In fact, there were a number of areas in which Nikki was a bit too well endowed.

But she certainly enjoyed herself up there. Her vibrancy was as strong and contagious as laughter. And Victor knew with absolute certainty that Nikki loved men. He knew that her womanly favors would have all the sparkle and substance of a hearty mug of beer. Men would have the feeling that they could drink fully from her cup and come away satisfied. Nikki exuded love of life at its most basic.

Even as he breathed in her sensuality, Victor was able to control his feelings. He was drawn to her, as any red-blooded male would be, but that very attraction constituted a loss of control —a loss that Victor would never allow. He wanted her, and he would have her. But he would win Nikki on his terms and only after he had established himself as the one in charge.

Satisfied with his resolve, Victor sat back and analyzed her performance. With some refinement to her act, she could be playing Las Vegas instead of this little country roadhouse outside Genoa City. Her earthy beauty wouldn't last forever, and she should be making money while she could. As her dance came to an end, the barflies hooted and hollered their approval. Victor slid off his stool and sauntered toward the back of the bar.

"Hey, Mac," the bartender snarled. "The broads' dressing rooms are back there. You can't—"

Victor laid a fifty-dollar bill on the bar and continued walking. Nikki was about to duck into a dressing room as Victor lifted the curtain leading to the back hallway.

"Nikki," he called.

Her brown eyes were cool as she studied him. Victor knew that she bleached her hair, and some would have found her brown eyes and dark brows disconcerting with her platinum locks, but he found the contrast exciting.

"Hey, Victor." She giggled flirtatiously. "No customers allowed back here."

"I paid the admission fee," Victor said as he stopped in front of her.

"Oh, a big spender." Her voice was low. She reached up to brush some lint off his shoulder.

His heartbeat increased, and Victor tried valiantly to control it. "What makes you think I'm a big spender?" he asked.

"Biff doesn't let anybody back here for less than a twenty." She turned into the dancers' dressing room. "Come on in," she said over her shoulder. "The girls enjoy seeing a live pair of pants once in a while."

He followed her, trying to suppress the disapproval that he felt once he saw the room. The half-naked women lounging around, some with their feet up on the dressing tables, didn't bother him. What he didn't like was the total disarray that greeted him: bits of clothing on the floor, open lipsticks and jars of face cream, and mirrors dull with cigarette smoke and years of accumulated grime.

Nikki retrieved a wad of gum that she had left on her table. "Wanna sit down?" she asked.

Victor shook his head.

"Did you catch my act?"

"Yes, I did," he answered, then lowered his voice. "I wanted to talk to you about that."

Her only reply was the snapping of her gum.

"I have some ideas on how you could improve your act."

"Oh, yeah," she snorted. "Well, before you go too far, I'd just like you to know that I don't work with animals, snakes, or chickens."

Victor smiled. "It's nothing like that, Nikki. You have too much class and talent for that."

"Oh?" Her tone was more interested.

"Why don't we have lunch tomorrow?" Victor said. "We can talk about it."

"Lunch?" She reached up to adjust a bikini strap that had slipped down over one shoulder. "I don't get up too early."

"A late lunch, then," Victor said. "I'll pick you up about one-thirty."

"I don't have to be here until five."

"Very good," Victor said. "That should give us enough time."

"I would think so," Nikki said, laughing. "Enough time for a lot."

Victor hurriedly left. Outside he paused to take a deep breath of the sharp, cold air. The snow crunched under his feet, and the clear night sky was ablaze with stars. There was something alluring beneath that woman's thin veneer. Nikki Reed was quickly getting into his blood.

Chapter Three

New Hopes

"What the hell is this?" Nikki demanded. "A kiddie meal?"

"That is the petite steak sandwich, madam." The waiter was almost whispering, but Nikki was unperturbed by his obvious embarrassment. That was his problem, not hers.

"Look at the size of his," she said, pointing at Victor's healthy-sized sandwich and the stack of cottage fries next to it.

"That is the man-sized steak sandwich," the waiter murmured. Although Nikki was aggravated, she almost laughed aloud at the way the waiter's eyebrows were nervously twitching.

Victor's face only wore an expression of comfortable amusement, so Nikki notched her voice up a few octaves. "This thing can't weigh more than two or three mosquitoes," she said, again pointing at the offending sandwich. "I could inhale it and not feel a thing. I'm a working girl, sweetheart. If I don't eat right, I'll be skin and bones in less than a week."

The waiter's face turned a brighter shade of crimson as Victor buried a chuckle in his napkin.

"Would you like me to take that back and bring you a man-sized steak sandwich?" the waiter asked through clenched teeth.

"Yeah, bring me one like that." She pointed at Victor's lunch. "And everything that goes with it." She picked up the petite sandwich and eyed it suspiciously. "I'll finish this little thing off while I'm waiting for my meal."

The waiter bowed, then hurried away. Victor was shaking with hearty laughter.

She took a bite out of the miniature sandwich and spoke through a mouthful of steak and bread. "No wonder they can afford to change the tablecloths after each party leaves. They sure don't give you much food for the money."

"Ambience can be expensive," Victor said.

Nikki glanced quickly around the dark paneled dining room with the wide spaces between tables. She wasn't sure that she would recognize ambience if she saw it, but a place like this would be expensive. Not only were their decorating costs high, but they had a lot of people standing around waiting for something to do.

"Madam."

"You're just in time," she said, stuffing a last potato in her mouth.

The waiter bowed and cleared her plate.

Nikki concentrated on eating her second sandwich.

Victor ate at a more leisurely pace, but he was finished at about the same time as she was. He had ordered a liter of rosé wine. Nikki sipped hers, then finished it off in a few swallows. She would have preferred a heavier red wine, but the one who paid the fiddler called the tune.

"Did you grow up in Genoa City?" Victor asked.

He sipped at his wine while Nikki poured herself a second glass and drank it thirstily.

"I was born in Chicago," Nikki answered. "We moved here when I was a baby. My sister's a doctor here in town, so I decided to settle for a while."

"Do you enjoy dancing?"

Nikki shrugged, bored with the conversation. "There are worse jobs." She gazed around the dining room. The clientele consisted primarily of men, well-groomed men, laughing and talking with the easy comfort that a full belly and an even fuller wallet gave a person.

"I'm going to have to tell the other girls about this place," Nikki said.

"You think they'll like the food?" Victor asked.

She shook her head and laughed. "If you want to hunt buffalo, you have to go where the buffalo roam." And there were a lot of rich buffalo here.

Victor smiled knowingly, so Nikki felt no

need to explain. That's what she liked about the man; he was pretty sharp. He wasn't bad looking, either.

"Have you tried other jobs?"

"Oh, yes," she said. "I picked cranberries, washed dishes, slung hash." Nikki shrugged. "I did a whole bunch of stuff."

"And now you've settled on dancing."

"You saw my act," she said. "I don't know if you'd call it dancing, but like I said, there are worse ways to make a buck."

"Have you tried any office jobs?" Victor asked.

Nikki waved her hand in disgust. "Not really," she said. "You have to dress like a nun, walk like a grandmother, and talk like a deacon. That's not for me."

Victor just nodded.

"Besides, the first thing they ask about is school and that kind of stuff."

"You didn't graduate from high school?"

"I finished my freshman year and part of my sophomore year."

He nodded again and stared at the wineglass he was slowly twirling between his fingers. Nikki pursed her lips and stared at her empty glass. This guy was starting to sound like a cop. She was getting thirsty again. She would even settle for another glass of that pink stuff.

"Have you had any training in dance?"

"Nope," she answered. "I watched some of the other girls, but I don't really do much. I just get up there and show the boys all the skin the law allows." She finished with a nervous laugh.

"You have a unique vitality," Victor said. "There's a certain electricity when you walk into a room. It happened even here." His hand swept the dining room. "I'm sure you noticed how the room quieted when you entered." A small smile came to his lips. "And, I might add, you were fully clothed."

"Yeah, I started noticing that when I was in the fourth or fifth grade," she said. "I think I'm in heat 365 days out of the year." She shrugged and, with a tired laugh, added, "It's 366 in leap year."

"I'd like to help you," Victor said.

Nikki suppressed her initial impulse to laugh out loud. "With what?" she asked.

"Dressing you."

Now Nikki had to snicker. "That's a new one for me. Guys usually want to help me undress."

Victor ignored her remark. "Posture, grooming, dancing lessons . . . whatever you need to make it to the top. I think you have the talent."

Nikki stared, more than a little frightened. Was this guy for real? "What's in it for you?" she asked.

"It will give me pleasure."

"I see," she said, breathing a small sigh of relief. He was like all the other man she'd met. Nikki knew she could handle him.

"What I mean," Victor explained, "is that I want you to think well of me."

Nikki let a broad smile cover her face. "Sure. That shouldn't be too hard."

"I'm going out for lunch," Greg told Chris. "I'm in the mood for a walk."

"Barbara says that if you give her a day's notice," Chris told him, "she can arrange for a longer lunch hour."

Greg clenched his teeth for a moment. His sister-in-law had been on his case almost constantly since his date with Barbara Lewis. Apparently Barbara had told Chris that she thoroughly enjoyed the evening, so now Chris was on his back, pushing him to take the woman out again. Barbara was a nice girl, but he just wasn't interested.

"Watch the office so it doesn't walk away," he said. "I'll be back soon, and then you can go to lunch."

"Don't worry about it," Chris replied. "I'm brown-bagging it today."

He nodded, then quickly stepped out the door before Chris could sing further praises of the sweet, marvelous Barbara.

Greg sighed as he buttoned his coat against the biting wind. Snow flurries whipped along the sidewalk. Greg couldn't blame anyone else for his failure with Barbara. He was still in love with Gwen, and his overwhelming obsession made it impossible to consider another relationship. He would bring nothing but grief to any other woman he tried to get involved with.

He would be doing Barbara a favor by staying away from her.

His feet had taken him to the edge of Genoa City's business district before he realized he was hungry. Bright red letters invited him to Hav-A-Snack, and he went inside, hung his coat on a rack, and took a seat at the counter where he could look out the window. Christmas was coming soon, and the streets were starting to fill with shoppers. He ordered the soup-and-sandwich special, then idly stared out at the passing throng. Glancing at the other side of the street, he caught sight of a redhead. She was turned toward the store windows, but her walk, her manner, her very essence were familiar to him. She paused and turned her head just slightly in his direction.

"Oh, my God!" he exclaimed, just as the waitress placed his soup and sandwich in front of him.

"What?" the waitress asked. "Is something wrong?"

But Greg barely heard her. He jumped to his feet and rushed outside, looking down the street at the people hurrying past. But the redhead was nowhere in sight.

"Hey," the waitress shouted, as she ran after him. "Come back here."

She caught up with him a few steps from the doorway. "You want to eat out here?" the waitress asked. "You're going to have to get your own table."

Greg reluctantly pulled his eyes back from their frantic search. "I'm sorry," he apologized. "I wasn't planning to stiff you. Here." He shoved several bills at the woman.

"The food's good, mister, but we aren't the Allegro. This is way too much," she said, handing some of the money back to him. "And you left your coat inside. Come back in and I'll give you your change."

"Keep it," Greg said, even as he was darting into the street.

Once across, he turned his eyes to the crowd again, forgetting all about the waitress and his abandoned lunch. He scanned the faces around him, pushing through the maze of people on the sidewalk. Damn. He was too late. He would never find her in this crowd.

His feet slowed as he silently berated himself. He was probably just being a fool, wanting to see Gwen so badly that now he saw her face in every redhead who passed by.

And the chances of this woman being Gwen were almost nonexistent. Gwen had long curly locks that framed her face; this woman's hair had been straight and short—just the way a nun would wear it, except this woman was dressed in ordinary clothes. And Gwen would be wearing a habit these days. She was a nun now, devoting her life to God.

Yet something in the glow on the woman's face, the brightness in her eyes, had reminded him of that summer of long ago: of the day when the thunderstorm had come and drenched both of them, when he and Gwen had made love in the old barn. Greg's eyes burned. *Damn the wind.* He wished he'd grabbed his coat before he took off. It felt like the North Pole, not the streets of Genoa City.

He shivered slightly and started searching again, though he had little hope of finding her. If it had been Gwen, why was she wearing street clothes? Maybe she had left the convent. Maybe she wasn't a nun anymore. That hope inspired him to continue his search.

After several treks up and down the streets, Greg knew that he had to give up. He was shivering violently now. Gwen was gone.

He turned back toward the Hav-A-Snack. Yes, she was gone and she would never return. That woman he had seen was just an apparition, the fruit of his need, a figment of his overactive imagination. Gwen was gone, period.

"Want your lunch now?" the waitress asked him.

Greg shook his head as he slipped on his overcoat.

"You paid enough for a whole slew of lunches," the waitress said.

"I'm not hungry," Greg snapped.

"How about a cup of coffee?" the woman asked. "You're shaking near to death."

Her solicitous manner softened Greg's heart, and he felt guilty at his churlishness. "Thank you," he said. "You're very kind, but I really have to be going."

"Come back again," she said. "My name's Shirley. I'm at this station every lunch hour. I figure I owe you at least one lunch."

The kindness had erased some of the bored tiredness from her voice, and Greg saw that the woman was quite young. If she fixed up her brown hair and put on a little makeup, she would be reasonably pretty.

"I'll remember that," he said.

The walk back to his office took him straight into the wind. He kept his head bowed and his hands thrust deep in his pockets. Tiny ice crystals formed on his eyelashes, but he was not really aware of the discomfort of his body. His soul felt much worse. Would he ever be able to purge himself of the memory of Gwen Sherman?

Nikki stopped her car at the curb, but left the engine running. Victor had told her to come to Janelle's at nine in the evening. He'd said he had a surprise for her, but the surprise could be that he'd been joking.

She looked up and down the dark, deserted street, then stared into the unlit window of Janelle's, one of the more expensive, fashionable boutiques in Genoa City. There were some lights on toward the back of the shop, but the place was obviously closed. The mannequins in the window returned Nikki's stare, hollow smiles on their lifeless lips.

The cynicism in Nikki's soul boiled up to match their blank stares. If he was actually here, what kind of surprise would Victor have in store for her? Nikki had had many surprises in her young lifetime, starting with her father's drunkenness when she'd come home from school after her first-grade Christmas pageant.

"Oh, what the hell. Might as well try the door," she muttered as she turned the ignition off. She was a big girl and well able to take care of herself. Victor Newman might be a little kinky, but he was also wealthy. That erased a lot of sins as far as she was concerned. She unwrapped a stick of gum and put it in her mouth, then sauntered up to the door. Victor's surprise had better be good; she was losing a whole night's pay for him.

Victor answered her knock. As she stepped inside, her expression quickly froze. Behind Victor stood another man, a little man with a nervous smile. A momentary wave of panic raced through Nikki. She didn't like group scenes.

"Nikki," Victor said, "this is Jason, the owner of Janelle's. Jason, this is Nikki Reed."

Jason bobbed his head several times and gave Nikki a weak handshake. Her panic was replaced by irritation. What was going on here?

"Let's go," Victor said brusquely as he slammed the door shut. "We have a lot of ground to cover tonight."

Jason silently hurried off toward the back of the boutique, and Victor took Nikki's arm, directing her to follow.

The back of the shop was a hodgepodge of material, sewing machines, and dress forms that presented a sharp contrast to the cool elegance of the sales floor.

"Come over here, please," Jason ordered, waving toward an open area under some bright lights.

Frowning slightly, Nikki strutted over to the floodlit area.

"Turn, turn," he said.

She wasn't sure what this was all about, but she did as she was ordered.

Jason grunted disapprovingly, shaking his head. "Now walk toward me."

When she was almost upon him, he ordered her to turn and walk away. She heard murmuring behind her.

"What the hell is going on?" she snapped at Victor.

"I told you I was going to help you," Victor said. "This is step one."

"There will have to be more steps after this, Mr. Newman," Jason twittered. "Many, many more."

"Shut up, Tweetie Bird," Nikki snarled.

"Ah, such spirit," Jason exclaimed, clapping his hands.

"I'd like this kept on a professional level," Victor snapped. "Nikki, keep quiet."

She glared at the smirking store owner, but did as Victor ordered. She'd give him a chance to show what he was up to before she walked out.

"Well, Jason," Victor said. "What's the verdict?"

"The structure has possibilities," Jason replied. "Good cheekbones, superb posture, but the shoulders are a trifle too broad."

"Why don't I chop a few inches off each one?" Nikki asked sarcastically.

Jason cast his eyes heavenward while Victor silenced her with a hard stare. Nikki's sarcasm dissolved beneath Victor's flinty gaze. This certainly wasn't going to be the kind of surprise she'd been expecting. She was being treated like a show horse. Considering some of the ways she'd been treated, it wasn't *too* bad. Perhaps she should try to behave for Victor's sake.

"Go on," Victor told Jason.

"Everything else is an absolute disaster, Mr. Newman. She paints her face like a dairy barn, the clothes are appalling, and her accessories —" He shook his head and clucked disapprovingly.

There was a limit to the amount of abuse Nikki would stand for. "I don't need this," she snapped.

"Relax," Victor told her.

"Relax, hell," Nikki shouted. "I'm losing more than fifty dollars to listen to these insults." Her lip wanted to quiver, but she was very practiced in controlling it. She'd learned long ago to never let her pain show. This was a mean world, and it wasn't a good idea to show weakness. Weak people got stomped on.

Victor merely held up a hand, and she swallowed her anger. She didn't like it, but it was Victor's show. Wherever Victor went, he probably always ran the show.

"Anything else?" he asked Jason.

The boutique owner shook his head. "Now we must start rebuilding." Then, seeing Nikki's frown, he quickly added, "We have a good foundation. In fact, the foundation is excellent."

Nikki continued to frown. What was this nonsense about foundations and rebuilding? They were talking about her as if she were an old house that they were going to renovate.

"Take your clothes off, Nikki," Victor ordered.

A hard smile came to her lips. It always came down to this. Now she was on familiar territory. She knew how to take care of herself in this situation. She kicked off her shoes, and dropped her skirt and blouse to the floor, all the while keeping her eyes on Victor. He was a hard man to read, but she thought she saw a glint come to his eyes when she peeled off her stockings very slowly.

She reached back to unhook her bra, but Victor stopped her. "Let's wait for that," he said.

Nikki shrugged, but then her irritation came back in full force. The boutique owner was coming toward her with a tape measure. Now what?

But all he did was take her measurements: bust, waist, hips, leg length.

"Does she need to lose any weight?" Victor asked.

Jason shrugged. "She's too heavy to be a model, but her shape is firm."

"So?" Victor asked.

The man giggled and Nikki felt like punchinghim. "Actually I think it adds to her image very well."

"Image?" Nikki asked.

"Oh, yes," Jason said. "There are women who would just die for a bit of your . . . your magnetism."

Magnetism? Nikki looked at Victor, but he was staring at the floor thoughtfully. "Dress her," he ordered Jason.

Nikki blinked in surprise. Dress her? She was going to be dressed in clothes from this place? That was beyond her wildest dreams, but she recovered her presence of mind in time to shout at the departing Jason, "I like red."

They waited in silence. Victor still seemed deep in thought, and Nikki didn't know what to say. Jason came back with a tan suit.

"I said red," Nikki reminded him in a harsh whisper that she hoped Victor wouldn't hear.

But Jason ignored her and worked silently. He helped her on with the suit and pinched and pinned it to fit her properly. Then with a wink he put a red scarf around her neck. Nikki almost smiled, but she held it back. No use being friendly until she knew why the hell Victor was doing this.

After gesturing for her to sit down, Jason measured her for her shoe size. "Big feet," he said. "Solid, too."

"The better to strut with," she whispered under her breath.

The shoes he brought back had a lower heel than Nikki was accustomed to, but they fit more comfortably than any shoes she'd ever owned, and they were as soft as gloves. Jason also put a bracelet on her left wrist, a chain made of heart-shaped gold links.

"Walk around a bit," Jason ordered her.

Nikki did as she was told. She smiled at her reflection in the mirror. She looked so . . . so classy. Was Victor going to buy her these clothes? She'd never worn anything so rich-looking, never thought she would own clothes like these. People would respect her when they saw her in this suit. She could go anywhere in Genoa City, anywhere in the country, and people would respect her. Waiters would seat her at the best tables, women wouldn't look down their noses at her, and men wouldn't leer. Well—she turned her back to the mirror and smiled over her shoulder at that view of herself—maybe they would leer more politely.

"There is only so much I can do," Jason said. "She needs Sonja's help. With her walk, especially." He shook his head sadly.

"What's the matter with my walk?" Nikki asked. But no one answered her.

"Take the clothes off," Victor barked.

Nikki stared, barely able to breathe. She felt as if she'd been kicked in the stomach. Was this it? What kind of game was Victor playing? Dressing her up to look better than she'd ever looked, dressing her like a lady, then taking it all away. What was wrong? Had he just discovered that "lady" was one term that didn't quite fit her? But she said nothing, just clenching her teeth and slowly stripping off her clothes. If the man wanted a show, he was going to get one. In fact, he would get the kind of performance that Nikki Reed always gave—the best.

The last thing she took off was the bracelet. She held it out to Jason, but Victor took it.

"This fits perfectly," he said, putting it back on her wrist. "I don't think it needs any alterations."

Alterations? Nikki stared into Victor's eyes. She didn't have to look at her wrist; she knew the bracelet looked beautiful.

"Jason will alter the suit," Victor was saying. "He'll put together a complete wardrobe for you. He'll have it ready for you tomorrow."

"Tomorrow?" Jason bleated.

"Tomorrow."

Victor's voice was determined and brooked no question, but his eyes were soft and gentle. Nikki felt a soft, warm smile creeping onto her lips. Her luck was changing. After all these years she'd finally found Santa Claus.

Chapter Four

Lesson Two

They had ridden in silence since they hit the edge of town. Nikki had chattered as usual until then, but once they'd passed Mill Edge Road she'd become tongue-tied. The snow-covered Wisconsin countryside looked so beautiful, like a picture from a calendar. Nikki knew it would have been dumb to tell him that, but she didn't know how to express the idea and make it sound intelligent. Victor had been spending a lot of time and money on her, and she wanted to impress him, but how?

"This is it," Victor said. "The Newman homestead."

They had been passing the same white crossbuck fence for almost a half-mile now. A matching gate was closed, but it magically opened when Victor pressed a few buttons on a remote-control device that he took from behind his sun visor. The gate closed after them as they drove up a long drive that wound through a forest of pine trees. Then suddenly they came to a clearing, and his house stood before them.

Nikki's eyes opened wide, and she was so breathless that she couldn't have spoken even if she'd known what to say. The style of the house was rustic, like a northwoods cabin, but it was also large and imposing.

"The stables are down there," Victor said with a gesture. "Do you like horses?"

"Oh, yes," Nikki exclaimed, finally finding her voice. "I've always loved to ride." Whenever the carnival had come to town she'd ridden the ponies until her father had said there wasn't any more money.

"Good," Victor said. "I do, too. Let's go see them."

Victor took her hand and they walked down to the barns, the cold snow crunching underfoot, trumpeting their arrival. At the stable, he opened the door with a flourish, and the cold, clean winter air was replaced by the warm, pungent odor of horses. Nikki held back, wrinklingher nose.

"Evenin', Mr. Newman. Evenin', ma'am." A short, wiry black man greeted them with a smile and a short bow.

"Hello," Nikki said hesitantly. The days were short in the winter, but she still found it hard to consider it evening when it wasn't quite four o'clock in the afternoon.

"How are all my beauties, George?" Victor asked. He walked up to the nearest stall and scratched the dark brown nose poking at him. "Are they ready for a little romp?"

"They're all full of vinegar." George laughed. "Exercise is always good for them."

Nikki hunched back and stared. These monsters were huge, much bigger than the carnival ponies had been. Was she really going to have to ride one of these dinosaurs in order to impress Victor?

"Nikki?" Victor's voice made her snap to attention. She turned to stare at him.

"What were you doing?" He laughed. "Daydreaming? I asked you if you wanted to go for a ride."

"Ride?"

"Yes. Horseback riding. You know, we put a saddle on one of these little guys and go trotting off on one of the trails. You said you liked riding horses."

"Oh, I do," Nikki stammered, smoothing down the red wool jumpsuit that Jason had designed and tailored for her. "It's just . . . I'm not dressed for it."

Victor shrugged. "We might be able to find you a pair of jeans and some old boots."

"No, no," Nikki insisted. "I haven't gone riding for a while, and I'd rather not today."

"Okay," Victor replied. "See you later, George."

The stableman touched his hand to his cap. As he bowed slightly to Nikki, she could see his eyes dancing. She clenched her jaws, and hurried outside. He knew. That man knew that she was faking it.

"Your car's gone," Nikki said, forcing herself to break the heavy silence they carried with them from the stables up to the house.

"The houseman put it in the garage." He opened the door for her, warmth and light spilling out of the house to greet them. "There's a bathroom at the end of the hall. Go freshen up; then meet me in the den. That's the room to your right as you go toward the bath."

Nikki nodded and went into the bathroom. She brushed her hair, wincing slightly. Since Jason had pointed it out to her a few days ago, she had been conscious of the contrast between the platinum hair and her dark eyebrows. After checking her lips, Nikki gazed longingly at the lipstick, but she left it in her purse. Jason had said that she was going to have to watch herself. It would take some time before she would get over her inclination to put on a double coat of paint, as Jason had put it in his snide way. She scurried across the hall into the den.

"Go back out into the hall." Victor's voice stopped her with an order. "And when you come in, make it a grand entrance."

Nikki stood still, her feet rooted to the floor.

"Let's go." Victor clapped his hands. "You can be a stripper or a dancer. The choice is yours."

"I'm sorry," she murmured and backed out. She should have known this was going to be another lesson, but Victor's motives were beyond her. If he liked her, why was he remaking her? And if he didn't like her, why was he spending a fortune on her?

It was too hard a puzzle to figure out, and Nikki just tossed her hair back, flinging her worries behind her also. Who was she to question Victor's motives? If he wanted to play teacher, she would let him. Putting up with a new wardrobe and learning to please him didn't seem too hard a task.

But a half-hour later, Nikki was no longer sure of that. She had lost count of the number of entrances she had made. It was probably closer to ten than to fifty, but none of them seemed to please Victor in the slightest. What did the man want? She'd been walking through doors all her life, and no one had ever complained before.

"Okay, sit down," Victor finally said. "You need more work, but you're doing much better. Your dance teacher will be better able to help you than I am."

Nikki slumped into a chair.

"Ah-ah-ah!" Victor shouted. "Dignity! Control! Never slouch. That presents a picture of defeat. And a man or woman of substance is never defeated."

Men and women of substance never had to scratch for pennies, Nikki wanted to say, but she forced a smile and sat up straight. After all, the customer was always right.

"Very good."

Victor's praise sent a new measure of vigor and determination flowing through her veins.

"Okay," Victor said as he poured some liquor into two large goblets. "We are going to pretend we are having a little cocktail party. It's cold out, and we have invited a few friends in for some brandy."

Nikki nodded as she looked at the partly filled glass Victor handed her. Normally he wasn't chintzy, but maybe the stuff was really expensive. She raised the glass and took a swallow.

"Now, the two main activities at a cocktail party are—"

"Wow!" Nikki exclaimed, gasping as she swallowed the liquid fire. "That'll take the hair off your chest."

Victor refilled her glass. "As I was starting to say, the main activities at a cocktail party are sipping and talking." He handed her the partially filled glass again. "Sip. Understand?"

The first belt she'd taken was still burning her pipes, so all Nikki could do was nod.

"Cocktail conversation has to be absolutely noncontroversial," Victor said. "Weather is usually a good topic. So you and I will talk a bit about the weather."

Nikki opened her mouth, but before any words could spill out Victor held up a hand to stop her. "Remember, sip first."

She sipped at the liquor in her glass and learned the value of drinking slowly and in small swallows. Instead of a burning flame, a pleasant warmth spread through her body.

"Boy, it's really cold out there."

Victor stared at her and after a long moment Nikki became uncomfortable. "What else do you want me to say?" she asked.

"Cocktail conversation must be stretched out," he said. "It's like sipping in reverse. How cold is it?"

"Cold enough to freeze a bear's chimes off." She laughed.

Victor frowned. "Chimes?"

"Yeah," Nikki replied. "It means—"

"I know. I know," he hastily assured her. He took a deep breath. "I want polite conversation, Nikki. *Polite.* Something that won't offend anybody."

"What's so upsetting about body talk?" she asked. She was getting tired of this. Everything she did seemed to be wrong.

"Try again," Victor said patiently. "How cold is it?"

"It's so cold my toes are numb."

"Good," he said. "That's a good start."

Nikki made a face. Yeah, if she was talking to a two-year-old.

"Now take another sip and continue."

By the time Victor let up on her, it was pitch dark outside, but fortunately they had changed from brandy to tea after her third glass. If they hadn't, she would have been dead drunk by now. As it was, she was dead tired, but she continued to sit up straight and smile politely.

Victor had been pressing her and criticizing her every move, but she wasn't upset. She had a lot to learn, and Victor wouldn't be taking this much time with her if he didn't like her. Actually he'd spent hours with her over the last few days. A lot of hours and a lot of money. It had to be more than merely liking her, she had realized about three snifters of tea back. He wouldn't go to all this trouble unless he was crazy about her. Her body warmed as she stole a glance at his stern face. It would be nice to go crazy with him.

Suddenly Victor stood up. "Relax," he told Nikki. "I'll be right back."

"I hope so," Nikki called after him. "I've got some hot talk about some cold weather just waiting to be said."

He didn't respond, and she just flopped back in the chair and looked at the blond paneling, Oriental rug, and Victor's big dark-leather chair. Boy, what a place! She could hardly wait to see the rest of it.

Her eyes misted and her mind drifted. Mrs. Victor Newman. Was that what he had in mind? She could see herself welcoming him home at night. Hugging him, kissing him, feeding him, and loving him. Then he would relax and sleep the night away. She would caress that tension out of his eyes.

And when he entertained, she would help. She would put the men at ease and keep them laughing. The men would have wives, but

Nikki pushed them from her mind. The men were the important ones; they made the business decisions. The women just stood around and—

"Here you go." He handed her a plate with a sandwich and potato chips.

"I could have made you something to eat," Nikki said.

Victor shrugged, sitting down with his own plate. "Then my housekeeper wouldn't have anything to do."

Nikki took a hefty bite of the sandwich and smiled. Mrs. Victor Newman didn't have to cook or do housework. All Mrs. Victor Newman had to do was keep her husband happy. Nikki knew there wasn't a man breathing whom she couldn't make happy.

She winked at Victor, but he was concentrating on his food. Nikki returned to her sandwich. All good things would come in time. She could hardly believe how her luck had changed since Victor came into her life.

"Soup and sandwich special?" the waitress asked.

"Yeah," Greg replied, continuing to gaze out the window. "That'll be fine."

"The sandwich is chicken salad," the waitress said. "We're not supposed to do it, but I can get the cook to give you ham instead."

Greg nodded absently.

"I don't know why they do things like that,"

she continued. "Most guys don't like salad sandwiches. And most of our customers are guys."

There weren't many stores out here on the edge of town, and initially Greg couldn't understand why there was such a traffic in front of the Hav-A-Snack. But as he walked around, looking for Gwen, he noticed that there were two city parking lots in the area. The lots in the center of town were crowded during the holidays, and the ones here on the edge of the business district were cheaper. Office workers also parked nearby. Did Gwen work in an office near here? That would mean she'd left the convent.

"You were here last week when we had tuna salad, weren't you? Why, I couldn't get my little brother to eat a tuna salad sandwich if I beat him with a stick."

Greg blinked in bewilderment at the young waitress. Was she talking about beating someone?

"I'll have Harry make you a ham sandwich," she said. "Like I said, we aren't supposed to do that, but Harry will do it for me. You want mayo on it?"

He shrugged, then he shook his head.

"How about mustard?"

He frowned. Greg really didn't care what he ate. "Sure—whatever you think."

Sighing in relief at the waitress's departure, Greg turned his attention back to the window. He'd come to this diner every day for almost a week now. He always came in around noon and took a seat at the counter so he could look out the window. And every day it was the same; he saw nothing, no trace of Gwen.

Had the redhead been an apparition? Had he just been dreaming? He rested his chin on his clenched fist. Maybe it was all a mistake. The woman's hair was short, and she had been wearing an ordinary cloth coat. But Gwen could have left the convent.

Greg furrowed his brow. More than likely she had just been an office worker, a stranger, and his imagination had transformed her into Gwen. This whole affair was dumb. He put his feet on the floor and tiredly prepared to leave.

"Here you are." The waitress placed the soup and sandwich in front of him. "I forgot to ask, so if you don't like the brown bread I'll get something else."

He sank back onto his stool. "No, this'll be fine."

Chewing the sandwich without tasting it, Greg went on staring out the window.

"Did she live in this neighborhood?"

He looked at the waitress's pensive face. "Live here? Who?"

"The woman you're looking for."

"Who said I was looking for a woman? I could be a policeman looking for a killer."

She laughed. It was a hearty laugh, but kind. "You can't be a cop," she said. "You look like too nice a guy."

"Thanks," Greg mumbled around his sandwich.

"It's a woman," she said firmly. "And you miss her a whole lot."

He paused a moment, then swallowed a bit of his sandwich. "You got your hair fixed a new way," he said. "It looks nice, real nice."

"Thanks," she said ruefully. "It cost me a twenty, and you're the first one who's noticed it."

"You want me to tell your boss how nice I think you look?" Greg asked.

"No." She waved, as if to dismiss the idea, and went off to pour another customer a cup of coffee. Greg concentrated on the pedestrian traffic outside. Gwen had just been a mirage, a figment of his imagination.

"Would you really?"

He brought his attention back to the waitress, who had returned.

"I mean, tell Harry that I look nice."

Greg clenched his jaw a moment. Now what had he gotten himself into? "Sure," he said. "You want me to do it now?"

She giggled. "No, let's give him another couple of days. See if he notices."

He nodded and dug his hand into his pocket for a tip. It was time to head back to the office. There was no sense in waiting around, mirages never reappeared—at least not in the same spot.

"Have a lot of work today?"

For some reason the young woman was

starting to irritate him. "Why do you ask?"

"You usually stay longer."

"Well, I can't today," he snapped.

Once he was outside, Greg was ashamed of himself. The waitress was just trying to be friendly. It wasn't her fault that he was getting so damned predictable. Hell, anybody would have noticed someone who ordered the same thing every day and then sat at the counter, staring out the window. He was lucky that she hadn't called the police. Considering it objectively, he supposed that his behavior seemed pretty damned weird. He was going to have to stop coming to the diner; that's all there was to it.

But what if the redhead really had been Gwen? If he stopped coming, how would he ever find her?

"Thank you, Father," Greg said, replacing the receiver as he forced himself to write some numbers on a notepad. He wasn't sure whether to smile or not.

"Who was that?" Chris asked, taking her scarf and coat off. She had returned from lunch earlier than he had expected.

"The Catholic chaplain from the hospital," Greg replied, slipping the paper under the corner of his blotter and out of sight. "One of his patients is an accident victim who might have grounds for a willful negligence suit. He wants me to come over for an interview."

"Want me to do it?" his sister-in-law asked. "I'm not that busy this afternoon."

"No."

"You have a meeting on the Bailer case in Judge Ryan's chambers at three, and you have to prepare for it."

"It's no problem," Greg snapped.

Chris looked intently at him, and Greg forced himself to relax. "This hospital thing could be complex. It involves a construction company and workmen's comp. I think it would be easier all around if I checked into it first."

"Okay." Chris shrugged, but a pout fought to establish itself on her face. "I was just trying to help."

"You do," he assured her. "I don't know what I'd do without you. I'd be running around like a rooster without his head."

"All right, Greg. You can stop buttering me up. I'm not mad anymore."

"Good." He put on his coat.

"But I want you to promise me something."

Greg stopped with the door open. "Yes?"

"I want you to stop babying me," Chris said. "If I'm going to be of any help to you, you're going to have to put me into the tougher situations. If I fail, then you should get a new assistant, and that's all there is to it."

"I'll remember that." He saluted her and went dashing down the stairs, feeling vaguely guilty about having lied to Chris.

He located his car and headed for a local

convent. On the way, Greg fought a battle between wanting to sing for joy that he'd found Gwen and wanting to wilt with unhappiness because the chaplain had told him that he thought Gwen was still in the convent. He tried hard to concentrate on his driving.

He should have realized that Gwen would have joined a convent that was close by. Why hadn't he thought to call the hospital chaplain before? The priest had counseled Gwen when she was in the hospital after Duke beat her, and the chaplain had, in fact, been the one who had helped her find God.

Maybe I've been putting the call off, Greg thought. Maybe he'd been afraid of finding out that she had joined a foreign mission and that he would never see her again.

Of course, he hadn't been too happy about lying to a priest, but he hadn't realized how stubborn the good father was going to get. Apparently he had promised Gwen that he would never disclose her whereabouts. Greg knew that was for her own protection, but he certainly wasn't going to hurt her, and Duke was in jail for a long, long time.

Still, Greg had had to tell the priest a story about a message from Gwen's dying mother that only he was authorized to deliver. The priest had wanted to call the convent to make sure Gwen was still there, but Greg had pointed out that they were running out of time.

Thinking of time, he glanced down at his speedometer and smiled. Time wasn't so short that he had to risk being arrested for speeding. He didn't want to be stopped right now. Greg knew that he was so high on love that the arresting officer would think he was on some controlled substance. But everything had to work out. He would see Gwen again, she would realize she loved him, and they would find a way to be together.

A sign indicated he should turn left to make his way to the convent. As Greg drove up the lane he saw some children sledding down a hill beyond the low stone wall. Inside those walls stood the convent, a hospital, a school for troubled children, and an orphanage. Given Gwen's childhood, she no doubt figured that she was well qualified to care for those youths.

Greg experienced a twinge of guilt at his own selfish desire to keep her for himself, but he quickly suppressed the feeling. She could accomplish so much more as the wife of a respected attorney.

He rang the front doorbell and waited, barely able to hear the shrieks and shouts of the sledding children above the beating of his heart. Was she still here? The priest said he hadn't kept in touch with Gwen; he knew only that she had come to this convent when she left the hospital. That was long enough ago so that much could have changed. Suddenly Greg's heart grew cold with fear. What if she wasn't here after all?

"Yes?" A bent crone of a nun in an old-fashioned habit had opened the door.

Greg pasted a pleasant smile on his face. "Good afternoon, Sister," he said. "I'm Greg Foster. I'm an attorney from Genoa City and—"

He stopped. The woman looked bewildered. It was possible she didn't hear well.

"I'm an attorney," he shouted. "From Genoa City."

"Genoa City," the nun shouted back. "It's that way." She pointed west.

He shook his head. "No, I—"

Irritation flashed across the nun's face. "Go back to the road," she shouted, gesturing broadly. "Then drive that way."

"I'm looking for a woman," Greg shouted almost at the top of his lungs.

The nun's frown grew deeper, and Greg felt his face grow warm as he hastened to explain. "A very special woman," he yelled. "Her name is Gwen Sherman."

The woman's face softened, but she shook her head.

He felt his heart falling to his shoes. "She's young and beautiful, like . . . like the morning sun. She has shiny, long red hair."

His throat hurt from the shouting, but it didn't compare to the pain in his heart when the nun shook her head again. "No one here like that," the nun said.

"Has she ever—"

"Sorry." The voice was firm. "There's no one like that here."

The door closed, and Greg shut his eyes very

hard so as not to let a single tear escape. He'd had such high hopes, and it was such a long way to fall down to reality.

Inside the convent a young nun came into the hallway and stopped to look over the older woman's shoulder at the figure barely visible through the stained-glass panes next to the door. "Who was that man, Sister Anthony?" she asked.

"Heh?"

"That man," the young woman repeated. "What did he want?"

Sister Anthony's face softened. "Ah, so sad. He is looking for a loved one, but he cannot find her. It is very sad."

The young nun went to a window in the next room and pulled aside the curtain to look out. The man's shoulders were slumped, and he was walking slowly back to his car. The young woman's heart stopped for a moment, then beat a slow, mournful refrain. Sister Anthony was right; it was sad. The young nun swallowed the lump that had risen in her throat. She wanted to call out to the man, but instead she let the curtain fall back across the window. She sighed, brushing her fingers through her short red hair.

"Sister Magdalene," a brisk voice called from the hallway. "Sister Magdalene, the doctor wants to see you immediately."

The young nun turned from the window and hurried across the worn carpet to the door.

Sister Anthony had disappeared, and a heavy-set nun was waiting in the hallway.

"Is it Ramón, Sister?" the young nun asked. "Has he spoken yet?"

The other nun shook her head slowly. "No, but now he has a fever. The doctor wants you to sit with the boy. You are his only comfort."

Sister Magdalene pushed Greg Foster from her mind as she hurried down the hall toward the hospital wing of the orphanage. Poor Ramón, she thought. He was so young and had so much to look forward to. If only he could be released from the torturous constraints of his silent prison. She would do anything to hear her name fall from his lips.

Chapter Five

Fading Dreams

"Are we going to meet anybody at the restaurant?" Nikki asked.

"No," Victor answered. "This is a dry run with us alone."

He took his eyes off the road for a moment and glanced at Nikki, curled up beside him, running her fingers over the leather upholstery. Victor had decided at the last minute to take the Mercedes sports coupe. It tended to attract attention, but he had wanted to see how Nikki would respond to the scrutiny of the public eye.

She was coming along well, this little spitfire. Her sensuous beauty still wanted to dominate his thoughts, and his body still burned with passion when she was near, but soon the training would be done. He would have transformed her into a suitable companion, just as he had done with Julia. Then, once he had established absolute control over who she was, he could satisfy other desires.

One of the front wheels skidded a little, and Victor quickly turned his full attention back to the road. The highways near his home had been plowed, but there were some icy spots on these narrower roads that could be dangerous if he wasn't alert.

He wore his usual solemn expression, but inside he felt quite good. Nikki was catching on. He'd picked her up late in the afternoon and driven her to his home for a quick run-through. She had done well. He knew she tired of the many practice sessions, but she was a tough lady; she had stood up to the pressure and performed admirably.

Her reaction to the new clothes he had given her was especially pleasing to him. She didn't gush or squeal as she had previously been prone to do. She simply thanked him and then calmly accepted the gifts. She was close to becoming the queen that he knew she could be.

"I've never been to a concert," Nikki said. "I've never been to the Allegro either."

Victor smiled. Even her speech was improving, and her voice had dropped in both pitch and volume. "Don't worry about it," he assured her. "I don't anticipate that you'll have any problems."

"I wasn't worrying about any," Nikki replied. "I was just thinking that I never wanted to go to concerts before. I always thought they'd be dull and stuffy. You know, for old people."

His smile disappeared, and taut lines appeared around his mouth. He took a deep breath and forced himself to relax. So his pupil wasn't quite finished yet. Rome wasn't built in a day.

Victor pulled up in front of the restaurant, then watched with approval as Nikki let the doorman help her out of the car, barely looking at him. She used to flirt outrageously with anything in pants. So far, so good. They moved into the dining room with an aura of dignity and decorum.

Following Victor's instructions, Nikki sat back and let him order their dinner. From the sound of the things Victor ordered, it was just as well. Nikki doubted she could have pronounced a single item on the menu, and she had no idea what any of it was.

Her confusion turned into distaste once the food came, and she felt like spitting. Frog legs and snails weren't exactly her favorite foods, although the frog legs weren't too bad; they tasted almost like chicken, just a lot skimpier. She would give two diamond pinky rings right now for a rare burger and a whole chicken, fried, with a side order of mashed potatoes drowned in brown gravy. Victor had said that a lady always left something on her plate, and that was easy to do with this junk.

"Would you like some dessert?" Victor asked.

Nikki smiled sweetly and replied in a gentle

voice, "No, thank you. I really couldn't swallow another bite." It was true. If he put a giant hot fudge sundae in front of her, she wouldn't swallow it; she would inhale it in one breath.

"Are you sure?" Victor persisted. "I understand that they have some interesting concoctions here."

Interesting concoctions? Probably something like lizards' eyes in chocolate sauce. She was learning quickly that one couldn't trust the weirdos who cooked in French restaurants. Nikki merely continued to smile and shake her head.

"Very well," he said, snapping his fingers for the check. "We'll be a little early for the concert, but not too bad."

Nikki didn't say anything as she searched Victor's face while he perused the check. This was their first real date, but he didn't seem too excited or even interested. Worry dampened the fires of her irritation. It hadn't been her idea to come to this stuffy place. Then to top it off they were going to spend a few hours listening to pompous music. She would have to take him to her place afterward and show him what a good time was. Nikki squashed her fear that Victor would refuse to come.

Outside she sucked in large gulps of the clear, cold air. "It's nice, and we have plenty of time," she said. "Why don't we walk?"

Victor's face remained blank as he signaled for his car. "The snow will just dirty the hem of your dress," he said. Once they'd settled into his car, he added, "And the salt from the street will dull the shine on your boots."

She turned away so that Victor wouldn't see the face she was making. Her grandmother, a farm woman, used to say, "Into everyone's life a few cow chips must fall." They rode to the concert hall in silence. If this was the type of evening Victor enjoyed, she would just have to get used to it. She would make some sacrifices, because he was important to her.

"We'll check our coats," Victor ordered as they made their way into the hall. "Then we'll mingle. Just hang on to my arm and remember all the things I've taught you."

Nikki straightened her shoulders, preparing to endure another test. She wondered when he would decide that she had passed and let them both relax.

Their coats were checked and Nikki was reaching for Victor's arm when the competitive radar within her sounded an alarm. Nikki turned to see a thin young woman with brownish hair bearing down on them.

"Victor," the woman breathed with a regal manner. "Victor, how wonderful to see you."

For the first time that evening, Victor's face broke into a genuine smile. But it was for this other woman, Nikki realized with anger. After all Nikki had done to try to please him, he only smiled when some other woman came around.

"Laurie," Victor said, taking the other woman's hand and lightly kissing it. "You are a vision of loveliness."

Nikki fought to keep a glower of jealousy from spilling over on her face. Vision of loveliness? That was true only if one liked his women skinny as a rail and pale as a ghost.

"Oh, Victor," the woman gushed. "You bring sunshine into a woman's day."

Victor continued holding her hand. "And how is Lance? Will he be here tonight?"

"Lance is fine, but he won't be able to make it. He left a message for me at the box office."

"Oh, no," Victor exclaimed. "Are you alone? Perhaps you can join us?" Then, almost as an afterthought, he pulled Nikki forward. "Laurie, I'd like you to meet a friend of mine, Nikki Reed. Nikki, this is Mrs. Laurie Prentiss."

"Good evening, Mrs. Prentiss," she said in a tone that she knew would please Victor. "It's a pleasure to meet you."

"Oh, yes," Laurie drawled but quickly turned to Victor. "We already have seats, and I don't know if it's possible to change."

"Let me take care of that," he said. "I'll be back in a moment, ladies."

The two women stared at each other for a long moment.

"I've heard a lot about you," Laurie said in a soft voice.

"That's nice," Nikki replied in the same genteel tone. "I wish I could say the same. I don't recall hearing anything about you." The blush of color in the woman's pale face fed Nikki's smile.

"It's all set," Victor interrupted, returning. "You'll be sitting with us."

"Oh, thank you, Victor," Laurie said, taking his arm. "Being with friends will make the concert so much more enjoyable."

Nikki bit back a snide reply and forced herself to be satisfied with Victor's other arm as the three of them made their way to their seats.

It took all of Nikki's strength and discipline to keep from screaming throughout the performance. Victor and Laurie spent the whole time whispering and smiling at each other. Out of all the pretentious noise the orchestra was making Nikki only recognized one song, the music they played at the beginning of the Lone Ranger movies. And since Victor had bought her boots for tonight she couldn't even slip her shoes off unobtrusively.

Her misery was compounded by Victor's obvious preference for Mrs. Laurie Prentiss. Nikki realized that once they escaped this dark hole she would have to come on strong or Victor would be gone. And once he was gone, she would be forced back to her old tricks, waving her fanny in front of the Bayou's slobberingclientele.

"Damn!" Greg cried. His eyes flew up from the brief in front of him as the office was plunged into pitch darkness. The room had no windows, so he didn't even have the light from the gray dusk outside.

"Do you really think you should be working late again?" The darkness enhanced the soft concern in his sister-in-law's voice.

"Chris," Greg protested wearily, "please turn the lights back on."

"Not until you promise me that you'll go out, have a nice dinner, and then go home and relax."

"I'm not hungry," he replied. "And I have no good reason for going home."

"How about if you come home and have dinner with Snapper and me, then?"

"I'm not hungry," he repeated.

The lights came back on, and Chris sat down in the upholstered chair in front of his desk. Maybe it was time to talk honestly to Greg and stop babying him.

"Haven't you got Nikki out of your system yet?" she asked. "You really don't have to worry about her. Rumor has it that Victor Newman is taking good care of her."

Greg laughed softly. "Women like Nikki don't need anybody to take care of them." He rubbed his eyes and then leaned back in his chair. "But in answer to your question, Nikki never got *into* my system."

"Oh," Chris said, disbelief making her voice cynical. "How silly of me to assume there was anything between the two of you. You were only husband and wife."

"I needed something, and Nikki needed something," Greg said. "We tried marriage and found our needs still unfulfilled. That was it."

Suddenly an awful thought struck her, erasingeverything but pity from her mind. "Oh, Greg. Please don't tell me it's still Gwen."

He closed his eyes and was silent for so long that she wondered whether he'd even heard her. Then he opened his eyes and she found herself staring into twin pools of pain.

"I saw her, Chris," he said slowly. "At least, I think I saw her, about two weeks ago."

Chris didn't say anything, but her curious expression urged him to go on.

"I went over to Fourth Street to get some lunch," he said. "I was staring out the window while I waited for my food."

She nodded.

"And I saw her go by." He shook his head in wonderment. "I swear to God it was Gwen. Her red hair was short, and her clothes were plain, but . . . but I'll never forget her face, Chris. Never in a million years."

"Did you speak to her?"

"I tried to follow her, but I lost her in the crowd," Greg replied. "You know how those holiday throngs are."

Chris waited for him to gather his thoughts and continue.

"Gwen had told me she was going into a convent, but this woman wasn't wearing a habit."

"She may have tried it and left," Chris said.

Greg shook his head. "If Gwen had left the order, I'm sure she would have come back to me." He thought he saw a cloud of doubt in

Chris's face. "I know you're skeptical, but I really believe she loved me. If it hadn't worked out in the convent, she would have come back to me."

"So where does that leave you now?" Chris asked quietly.

"Confused. If she is a nun, why wasn't she dressed like one? If she's not, why hasn't she called me?"

"You may never know the truth," she pointed out.

He shrugged off the thoughts that were plaguing him and looked up at her. "Do you remember that day last week when I called the Catholic chaplain at the hospital?"

Chris nodded.

"That call wasn't about an accident victim, Chris; it was about Gwen. At first the priest wouldn't tell me where she went, but I gave him a story and he told me."

Disapproval flashed on her face.

"I was desperate," he explained.

"I'm not judging you," Chris said.

"That's not what I read in your expression."

"Greg, the Chinese say that a friend's face mirrors our own feelings."

He stared at the floor for a moment, then took a deep breath and slowly let it out. "The priest said she went to a convent just outside the city. I almost jumped for joy. She was close by and I could go to see her."

"Did you go check it out?" she asked.

He nodded. "But she wasn't there. They said they'd never heard of her."

"Maybe the priest gave *you* a story," Chris said.

Greg laughed bitterly. "A man of God doing a thing like that?" When Chris didn't reply, he added, "Yeah, I thought of that."

"Maybe she left the convent and the priest didn't know it."

"I thought of that, too."

"Maybe she's changed her name and no one knows what her real name is."

"I've thought of all that," Greg said, his voice rising. "I've thought of a whole bunch of things, but none of them is getting me any closer to Gwen."

They sat in silence, drifting on the tides of time that spoke in the ticking of a clock instead of the lapping of waves.

Chris finally broke the silence. "You haven't moved since she left you."

"So what?" Greg replied.

"So if she wanted to contact you, she could have. But she hasn't, Greg. That can only mean that she doesn't want to." Chris leaned forward and wagged her finger for emphasis. "Whether she's a nun or not, she seems to have no desire to see you."

"You don't know that." A momentary shot of anger made him raise his voice.

Chris's heart ached at the unhappiness in his eyes, and she didn't want him to be hurt any more. "Oh, Greg," she pleaded. "Let her go. Gwen left of her own free will. Don't waste your life chasing a dream that was never meant to be."

"I want to see her," Greg said. "I want to talk to her. She's been away. She's had time to think, to heal."

Although he sensed Chris's reluctance, he pushed on.

"I have to know what her feelings are. I won't have any peace until I know if she's truly happy with her choice."

"Oh, Greg." Chris's face had grown soft and tender.

"I have to find her," he said. "Will you help me?"

"Will you go home?" she asked. "And have a good dinner and rest?"

Greg laughed and nodded. Chris rose and, as he got to his feet and came around the desk, turned off the light again.

"I'll do what I can, Greg," she promised as they left the office together. "But don't get your hopes up. Maybe it's better if you never find her."

"Don't say that, Chris," he shot back. "That woman is my whole life. I have to find her."

Nikki was glad that Laurie had driven to the concert by herself so she could drive herself home. Laurie had stolen enough of Victor's attention to last her a month of Sundays, and

Nikki was not going to let her get one more moment of it, not if she could stop it. However, the drive to Nikki's home, alone with Victor, was heavy with silence. He seemed in a dark mood, while Nikki was about to explode from all those hours of sitting quietly and restraining her ebullient energy. What could she do to make him forget his moodiness and smile at her the way he had smiled at Laurie?

He pulled to a stop in front of her apartment house. "Good night, Nikki," he said. "You did very well tonight."

Was this how he would have dropped Laurie off if he'd taken her home? Would he have said good-bye to her at the curb? Although she was seething inside, Nikki knew better than to start an argument with Victor. That wasn't the way to reach him.

"I couldn't have done it without your help," she cooed, her voice as sweet as sugar. "Why don't you come in so I can thank you properly?"

"There's no need for that. Besides, I'm—"

"If you don't come in, I'll let all the air out of your tires. Anyway, you've never seen my place."

Ignoring the tension that tightened Victor's face as he got out of the car, she pulled him inside the building and down the hallway to her apartment. She let go of him only long enough to unlock her door.

"I decorated it myself," Nikki said, indicating

the one-bedroom apartment with a sweep of her hand.

Victor solemnly looked at the cluttered living room. A heavy multicolored wool afghan covered the sofa, obviously hiding the holes in the seat cushions. Small pillows filled the armchair, and big pillows were scattered on the floor. Mismatched shoes peeked out from under the coffee table.

"How would you describe this decor?" Victor asked.

She wrinkled her nose at the humorless tone in his voice. "Real comfortable."

Nikki went into the kitchen and dropped her coat on the table, alongside a rabbit fur jacket that was already lying there. "Good," she murmured to herself as she checked the cabinet and saw that she wouldn't have to wash any glasses.

"The bathroom's through here," she called out. "Go ahead if you have to tinkle or anything. I'm going to change into something comfortable."

Victor didn't move, and Nikki shrugged. In her bedroom she stripped off her formal clothes in world-record speed, flinging the various garments onto the floor. Nikki smiled in relief as she wiggled her toes. Being a lady brought a load of discomfort with it.

But Nikki was not a contemplative sort, and she stretched her arms up high as her muscles exulted and cried out in their freedom. Then she rubbed the bottoms of her feet on the shag rug while she searched through the piles of clothing that cluttered the bed. She grunted happily when she found a short terry-cloth bathrobe.

Nikki smiled in the mirror as she wrapped the red robe around herself. She called the garment her drop cloth because it came off in a flash when a man wanted her. On impulse, she looked around for her high-heeled sandals, but quickly gave up. Those high-heeled boots had been punishment enough for her feet for one night. They'd earned their freedom.

She brushed her hair. Poor Victor was a little tense. Well, little Nikki had the medicine for that. He wouldn't be uptight for long. Nikki had been practicing the art of relaxing the male animal for a long time. There wasn't a man alive that she couldn't loosen up.

"How about a little drink?" she asked as she walked back into the kitchen.

"I really should be going," Victor replied.

She tossed ice cubes into two clean glasses and splashed some whiskey on them. "I don't have any soda," she said, adding water to the drinks. "Water okay?"

He didn't answer, and Nikki smiled at him as he stood in the doorway. Silence was consent.

"Here you go, sweets."

Nikki handed Victor the glass, then pressed her body to his as she led him into the living room.

"Aren't you warm in that?" She put both

their drinks on an end table. "Here," she said, pulling off his coat. "Make yourself comfortable." She threw his coat on the couch.

Victor's face retained its dark mask. A flash of irritation dashed through Nikki. She wondered what, if anything, would loosen this man up. But then she squared her shoulders and went forth to meet the challenge.

Victor fought to ignore her suggestive manner. One look at her in that short robe and his body wanted to burst into flame, to consume hers in a wild conflagration. But he could fight it. He would not let her body control his actions.

She grabbed one of the glasses off the table, drank some of the whiskey, and handed the rest to Victor. "You don't have to worry about germs," she said in answer to his dour glance. "That stuff will kill any bug."

He sipped a bit of the drink, then set it on the end table. Nikki snuggled up to him, wiggling her voluptuous body. He felt his iron restraint slipping. Her perfume, which he had chosen, tickled his senses. The fire in him was growing, threatening to burn out of control.

"I really have to go, Nikki." In seconds he got to his feet, leaving her alone on the floor. She wanted to hold him, to keep him next to her, but shame, shame that she had to clutch at a man, stripped her of her strength.

She remained on the sofa while he slipped on his coat. "I'll call you," he said, then was gone.

"Who gives a tinker's dam?" she muttered, hot tears streaming down her cheeks. They were tears of bruised pride, tears of shame, tears of need, a deep, aching physical need that had never gone unsatisfied in her life. Nikki cried, and the bitter wrenching sobs tore at her soul.

Chapter Six

Love's Growing Hungers

The words were swimming before his eyes, and soon Greg couldn't even distinguish the individual letters typed on the pages. He buried his face in his hands, then quickly dropped them and lifted his eyes to stare at the wall. With his eyes closed, he had clearly seen Gwen's smiling face, framed in long red curls. Now he could only see an outline floating on the opposite wall.

Oh, Lord, where had she gone? Why couldn't he just find her and feel alive again?

Chris appeared, rapping lightly on his open door. "Miss Roberts is here," she said.

"Roberts?"

Greg clawed at the clouds enveloping his mind, fighting to return to earth and reality.

"Yes," Chris answered. She came into his office, beckoning for someone to follow her. He quickly recognized the buxom black woman who came in. Miss Roberts worked with the juvenile offenders whom Greg defended. "She came in to discuss Ricky Thomas."

Ricky Thomas . . . thirteen and already a master car thief. Greg came back to reality, a painful reality, with a thud. He couldn't help Ricky Thomas overcome his legacy of poverty and despair. He couldn't find Gwen. He couldn't do a damn thing. He felt totally useless.

"What the hell is there to discuss?" he said, standing up. "Put him in jail and throw away the key. That's what he's destined for, and locking him up now will save all of us the trouble of going through useless motions." He stormed out of the office.

The slammed door echoed throughout the sparse suite of offices. Chris hung her head, too embarrassed to face the caseworker.

"Poor Greg," Miss Roberts said. "He must be carrying a heavy load."

Estelle Roberts was the same age as Chris and Greg, but she had grown up in harsh circumstances, and she now spent her days and many nights helping people conquer the same environment that she herself had beaten. Her eyes had a soft nonjudgmental light to them. Chris felt the other woman's understanding wrap around her like a soft blanket.

"He's usually so levelheaded," Chris said, shaking her head.

Estelle Roberts laughed softly. "Chris, it isn't human to be perfect."

"He's in love with a woman," Chris said. "In

fact, he's obsessed with her." Chris stopped, not wanting to burden her visitor with Greg's problems.

"Is it Nikki?" Estelle asked.

The caseworker's smile was so understanding and her question was so direct that Chris was compelled to reach out and hug Estelle. If Chris ever found herself in trouble, there wasn't anyone else in the world she would rather have in her corner than Estelle Roberts.

Chris suddenly felt embarrassed and let go, settling back into her chair.

"No, he knew this woman before he married Nikki. Her name is Gwen Sherman."

"Oh, yes," Estelle said. "She's the one who sent Duke up the river. She's a super lady in my book."

"Yes, she is," Chris agreed. She fell silent for several moments and then added, "She entered a convent. The chaplain at the hospital told Greg that it was the one east of town."

The caseworker's face turned thoughtful. "What does Gwen Sherman look like?" she asked. "I've never met her."

"You've probably never seen her either. Greg wouldn't let her be photographed during the trial," Chris said. "At the time, her hair was long and red. Her face was bright and good looking; even without makeup she had a fresh, healthy look."

"Hmm."

Chris laughed ruefully. "I know. It sounds like an ad for clean living. She's of medium height, well built and strong. She had to be strong to endure the punishment her body took."

"Yes," Estelle said. "I heard that her pimp gave her quite a beating."

"She was also heavily into drugs," Chris added. She paused a moment and thought about the information she had just furnished. "I'm sure what I just told you could fit several women. I guess what I remember about her most was her smile. She was an optimistic person even in the worst of situations."

"Sounds like Sister Magdalene," Estelle said.

"Who?"

"There is a novice in that convent you mentioned. She's called Sister Magdalene, for some reason, even though she hasn't taken her vows yet. I think she's the only one there with red hair, although it isn't long and curly anymore. The novices have it cut short, sort of in a pageboy."

"Are you certain?" Chris asked.

The caseworker nodded. "Sure am. All of us know Sister Magdalene. She works in the center for abused children. That girl always volunteers for the worst cases and brings them around. I guess with her background she can understand what those kids have been through and not be shocked by it."

"Oh, Lord," Chris said with a sigh. "I wonder if I should tell Greg."

"Do you have a choice?"

"No," Chris replied. "I'd want to know if I were in his shoes." She paused a moment and then smiled at Estelle Roberts. "I don't know how we can thank you."

"Don't give up on Ricky Thomas," she said with quiet conviction. Then without another word, she stood up and left.

Chris sat on pins and needles for the next hour or so. She called any number of places where she thought Greg might have gone, but no one had seen him. If he was walking the streets, she would just have to wait until he returned.

Finally the door opened and Greg slouched in. "I see Miss Roberts left," he said as he fell heavily into his chair. "Can't say I blame her. I was really out of line. I hope you offered her my apologies."

"No, I—"

"You're right," Greg said as he reached for the phone. "I was the fool, so I should do the apologizing."

"Greg. She told me where Gwen is."

He dialed two more numbers before his gray face hardened. He stared fixedly at Chris, holding the receiver in midair.

"I described her, and Estelle says that she knows her very well. Her name is Sister Magdalene now, and she's at that convent you visited."

Greg slowly replaced the receiver and put his hands in his lap so that his desk would hide their tremor.

"She works in their center for abused children."

"So the priest was right," Greg said. The trembling moved up into his shoulders. "She *is* there."

Slowly the hardness in his face receded and despair returned. "She was probably there the day I asked about her." The hopelessness turned to pain, and his eyes gleamed with moisture. "She doesn't want to see me. That's why they told me she wasn't there."

"You don't know that," Chris argued.

"Why else would they tell me she wasn't there?"

Chris shook her head. "I don't know, but there's only one way to find out."

Nikki paused at the carved oak doors and took a deep breath. The gold lettering looked as if it had been done by the same guy who did the engravingon elegant jewelry. As she read the name, Chancellor Industries, she wondered if it would ever be Newman Industries.

Nikki took another deep breath. Madame Sonja, her dance instructor, had told her that men figured the harder it swung, the cheaper it was. And she knew that Victor wanted nothing but first class. Nikki opened the door and sauntered in with almost no sway to her hips.

"May I help you?" the small, thin woman behind the desk asked.

"I doubt it," Nikki said as she went on to the

executive offices. She knew where Victor's office was; he'd shown it to her one night.

Another skinny woman sat at a desk outside Victor's office. This one had dull brown hair. She was mumbling into the phone and gave Nikki the fish eye as she headed for Victor's door.

The woman stood up and positioned herself in Nikki's path. "May I help you?" she asked coldly.

Nikki paused and looked the woman up and down. She just smiled and moved to go around the woman, who again attempted to block her way.

"These are executive offices," the secretary said.

"I know," Nikki replied. "I'm going to see Victor."

"Do you have an appointment?"

The woman was acting like an armed guard. "Get real," Nikki snapped, pushing past her.

The secretary chased her. "If you don't have an appointment, you can't go any farther."

Nikki smiled. She was getting tired of the kids' game. "I'm in a bit of a hurry," she said. "But if you want to go a quick round I'll be glad to take care of you."

The woman put a quivering hand up to her lips. "I'll call security," she squeaked.

"Better check with Victor first," Nikki growled as she walked by.

"Mr. Newman has a very private call," she called after her.

But Nikki just walked into his office. He was at his desk, talking on the phone. "Hi, Victor."

He silently waved her to a chair and concentrated on his call. "Is Lance out of town again?"

The tone of Victor's voice was easy and comfortable, but it froze Nikki's heart in fear. Would he talk that way to someone named Lance? No, he was talking *about* Lance, to someone else.

"Dinner would be fine, Laurie. I'd enjoy it very much."

Laurie! It was that long thin glass of ice water from the concert. Why was Victor going to have dinner with her? Nikki gritted her teeth. What could that woman give him? Did he like ice goddesses instead of warm flesh and blood?

"Outstanding," Victor said. "Seven o'clock would be quite suitable. I'll make the reservations and I'll call for you around six forty-ive."

Call for her? Nikki's hands clenched into tight fists. Give her two minutes with that bag of bones and there wouldn't be enough left for a Pekingese to pick over. What was wrong with her that Victor was picking Laurie Prentiss instead of Nikki Reed? Had she failed one of his tests? Didn't he love her after all?

Victor hung up the telephone and turned his attention to Nikki. "How are you this fine afternoon?" he asked. "Have we had enough snow for you?"

"It doesn't matter to me," Nikki remarked sullenly. "I don't use it for anything. It just sits there."

He stared at her for a long moment, and Nikki tightened her muscles to keep from shivering. The temperature in Victor's eyes would frost a blast furnace.

"How droll," he finally said with a short laugh. "I was just making small talk."

Nikki swallowed hard. She'd let herself be flustered at the thought of Victor going out with Mrs. Society, and that was no way to win the old ball game. She forced herself to relax. If he wanted to play games, fine. She'd been playing for a long time now.

"Actually, I'm a little tired." She fixed a sweet-little-girl smile on her face. "The guys at the club kept calling me back again and again last night. I mean, I was ready to drop."

His face was a blank page as he stared at her impassively. She squashed the feeling of desperation that wanted to surface and put a giggle in its place. "They almost had to call out the National Guard to escort me safely back to the dressing rooms."

"Hm," Victor grunted. "That's interesting. Did you include some of the steps Madame Sonja taught you?"

"Yeah." Nikki's tone was slightly belligerent, but her feelings were somewhat uncertain.

"Excellent. I'm glad to hear that things are really starting to move."

"Yeah." Her tone had become very uncertain.

"Yes," he said, correcting her. His voice was vigorous and commanding. "You appear to be progressing right on schedule. You're growing into a lady, Nikki."

"Is that right? Maybe I should go on a diet."

Victor laughed heartily. "Ah, Nikki. Dear Nikki. You have such a dry sense of humor. Don't ever let anybody change that."

"I won't," she muttered.

"Who knows," he went on. "When you're older and the sands of your personality have shifted with time, you may become a comedienne. You might want to work on that. It's always good to have something to fall back on."

Why would she need something to fall back on if she was married to him? Nikki could feel a dark mood falling over her. Victor didn't seem to care for her at all.

"I'll talk to Madame Sonja today or tomorrow," Victor said. "I think we're ready to add a few new routines and costumes. Another few weeks and you should be ready for Chicago. Then it's Las Vegas and on to Hollywood."

She didn't care about Chicago or Las Vegas —not when he was here in Genoa City. But all she could do was nod.

"I'm afraid I have to run along," he said with a quick glance at his watch. "I have a meeting with our marketing staff. I'll call you in the next few days."

Nikki sat there for a long moment after the door slammed behind her. Victor hadn't even given her time to invite him out for lunch. He didn't care for her. She was just a toy to him, a plaything, not a playmate. A single tear rolled down her left cheek.

Gritting her teeth, she tried to ward off the horrible, dejected feeling. She took her compact from her purse. Those skinny secretaries weren't going to see her with her face all smudged up. She wasn't through fighting, not by a long shot.

Each year the convent opened its grounds and chapel to the public for Advent services, the traditional ritual of song and prayer in preparation for celebrating the birthday of Jesus. Since it was a Tuesday evening, the crowds were small and Greg had no trouble finding a parkingplace in the lot. It was also still quite early.

He went first to the chapel and paused for a moment to study the statues of smiling angels and solemn saints. Two elderly nuns were bustling around the sanctuary, lighting candles and spreading a white cloth on the altar. Most likely the other sisters would not arrive until the services were about to start. He was sure that all of the nuns would be there, because the sisters' choir was one of the highlights of the Advent services. People of all denominations came from near and far just to listen to the choir.

He wandered outside to wait, looking around at the various buildings that stood on the grounds. He wondered which one was the convent. That would probably be the one that Gwen would come from.

Or she might come from the hospital or the children's quarters, he thought. If she did that, she wouldn't have time to freshen up, but did a nun need to freshen up? Didn't they renounce all such vanities? But weren't nuns still women?

His head reeled from all the questions. Greg rubbed his eyes. Even if he was waiting on the right path as Gwen made her way to the chapel, she would probably be walking with a whole group of sisters. Greg had heard somewhere that this order of nuns was extremely progressive, but he still felt apprehensive about approachingGwen when she was with the other sisters. He wasn't going to make any progress unless he got himself under control.

Finally, he chose a grove of trees within a large circular walk that seemed to lead from the chapel to the other buildings. Around the edge of the grove were carved scenes of the suffering Christ, the stations of the cross. The grove offered an advantage in that all the trees had shed their leaves for the winter. One could see the entire path from anyplace in the circle.

It began to snow heavily, and he cursed his luck. The snow would obscure his vision, and Gwen might slip right by him.

Happy, chattering female voices alerted him, and he watched the walk intently. Several nuns were making their way toward the chapel. They laughed and talked like a group of high school girls. A sliver of guilt slipped into his heart.

Those women sounded so cheerful and happy. Did he have a right to ask Gwen to give up that happiness?

Clenching his jaw, Greg stared at the sisters, who were on the other side of the grove. Gwen wasn't among them. Slowly, he paced along, pretending to study the next carved scene. Other groups came by, but still there was no Gwen. There were women in ordinary street clothes among some of the groups, probably women considering joining the order. He wondered what stories they brought with them. Greg doubted that any had the depth of tragedy that Gwen's had.

As he neared the edge of the grove, Greg wondered what he should do next. He wanted to meet Gwen alone. Somehow he didn't feel that approaching her in church, with a large number of her peers, was a good idea. But he hadn't seen her, so maybe she wasn't going to the chapel tonight. Maybe she couldn't sing. He laughed at that thought. Gwen had many talents. If she wasn't here, it was more likely that she was ill.

He wandered aimlessly for a while, then stared at the carving of Christ hanging on the cross. Should he go into the church or not? It would look suspicious if he lingered here too long, especially in what was now a heavy snowfall. No one was that pious. But he really didn't know if he could stand to sit quietly in a church while Gwen happily raised her voice in song. Maybe he should just pack it in and go home. God appeared to be less than enthusiastic about them getting together.

He turned toward the parking lot, but stopped to watch a solitary figure hurrying down the path. She was not dressed in a nun's habit. His shoes were soaked through, the bottoms of his trousers were wet, and melted snow trickled down the back of his neck to send a chill through his body. Yet it was minor in comparison with the chill he felt in his heart as she drew closer. Unruly red hair was peaking out from under her scarf. Greg's heart faltered a moment and then stopped. It was Gwen.

Chapter Seven

Dreams Come True

"Gwen?" Greg said quietly, almost disbelievingly.

She paused and blinked at the hunched figure standing before her. He wore no hat, and his hands were in his pockets. His face was obscured by the dusk and the heavy snow, but his pain showed through like a campfire in the night.

"Hello, Greg," she said.

He stepped forward and took her gloved hands in his bare ones. Although his eyes were shining, Gwen still could not read them. Was he moved by anguish, need, or fear?

"It really is you." His voice was almost a whisper. "I can hardly believe it." A choke had crept into his voice. "After all this time it really is you."

Gwen knew that she should pull her hands away, but she couldn't bring herself to do it. She had dedicated her life to God, but Greg's touch had stirred up a cauldron of old feelings. She had to stay with him for just a moment.

"Have I changed so much that you had difficulty recognizing me?" she asked.

"Not really," he said. "I was just surprised."

Gwen laughed. "Surprised? Why? Didn't you think they let us walk around the outside world?"

"I guess I did think something like that." He wore a thoughtful expression for a moment. "What really threw me was that you aren't wearing a nun's outfit."

"It's called a habit," Gwen said. "Novices in our order don't wear habits when they go out in the world."

His puzzled expression prompted her to explain further. "A novice is a nun who hasn't yet taken her final vows." His expression was only slightly less puzzled. "A novice is free to leave the order whenever she wants."

The puzzlement disappeared, but in its wake it left a collage of emotions on his features: hope, fear, uncertainty, and a bit of joy. "Your hair is shorter," Greg said, breaking the silence after a long moment. "But you're still as beautiful as ever."

A warm feeling of pleasure washed over her before she knew what was happening. Gwen frowned as she fought to drive it away. The old vanity had not yet been stamped out. She pulled slightly at her hands, but Greg held on all the tighter.

"You were on Fourth Street a few weeks ago, weren't you?"

Relaxing her hands, Gwen just stood there and looked deep into Greg's eyes. An innocent, earnest expression covered his face, and his eyes were full of pleading and hope. She could answer negatively, deny that he had ever seen her, even deny that she had ever thought of seeing him again. That would send him off, perhaps to search for another redhead. It would end this whole affair. Greg would be disappointed, but he would never come back again.

"Yes. In front of the Hav-A-Snack." She stood very still, shocked as she heard the answer pour out of her mouth. Her heart slowed and she held her breath, fearfully wondering what other words would escape. "I saw you when you came to the convent the following week."

The pain in his eyes disappeared, buried in a blinding light of pure joy. Oh, dear, Gwen thought. Now she'd gone and done it. Her heart sank even further. She'd done an unforgivable thing. She'd given him hope, even though his dream could never be fulfilled.

"I have to go, Greg. They're about ready to start the services." She tried to pull her hands away.

His grip became stronger to match hers. "Are you going to sing?" he asked.

"I'm part of the choir," she replied.

"The best part, no doubt."

Gwen pulled back quickly and hard. She reclaimed her hands and squeezed them into tight fists. She'd fought so hard since she came to the convent. She'd cut her hair to fight vanity, she'd closed her ears to all praise to develop the virtue of humility, and she'd driven her body until it desired only food and rest.

Now Greg had reentered her life. He admired her, praised her, and still desired her. Her spirit reached out to him.

Gwen was filled with fear. If her soul had capitulated so quickly, could her body be far behind? First it would warm to his glance, then it would yearn for his touch. Soon her body would lust for his, and then Satan would have her in his grasp again. . . .

Organ music wafted out across the still, white grounds. "I'm sorry, Greg," she said. "I really must go now."

"When can I see you again?"

"Come to the service. I'm in the last row, second from your left."

"That's not what I mean," he said. "I want to talk to you."

"Greg, please—"

"We have to talk." The pain had returned to his eyes with a vengeance. He was starting to shiver from the wet and the cold.

"Greg," she said quietly, "some things cannot be."

"I tried to forget you," he cried. "Honest to God, I tried. I'm working longer hours. I was even married for a while. But nothing works. I think of you all the time."

Her feet wanted to flee, but her heart wanted to stay. The music from the chapel grew louder, pulling at her conscience. "I'll call you," she said.

"Give me your number," Greg said. "Please."

"I will call you," Gwen said, starting to move away.

"When?" he asked, afraid to let her go, afraid that this would all prove to have been a dream.

Her feet moved faster. The ceremony would start soon. She had to be in her place.

"Gwen." It was a cry of anguish. "How do I know you'll call?"

"You have my word," she shouted. "My word as a woman of God."

Gwen turned and ran to the chapel. Snowflakes quickly melted in the hot river of tears that flowed down her cheeks. She had fought such a difficult battle. Gwen feared that she had no strength left. *Please Lord,* she prayed in silent anguish, *take this pain from me.*

Greg stayed there for a while, shivering and cold. Then he decided that listening to Gwen sing in a choir was better than nothing. He had taken a step toward the chapel when suddenly it struck him. She had said she was a novice, and novices were free to leave—free to leave at any time. Did that mean . . . ?

With a measure of hope he turned to walk

toward his car. Hope was such a treacherous thing; it could feed a man's soul and give it strength. But it could also act like a gas, pumpingthe soul up, setting it up to explode and fall to earth at the slightest buffeting. Greg didn't want to frighten Gwen by pursuing her. He would go home and maybe Gwen would call. She had given her word. His head was starting to ache by the time he found his car. He loved her so much it hurt.

"I used to love your salmon," Laurie told the waiter, "but the last time I had it the sauce was too tart."

"Yes, yes," the man said. "Pierre was trying a little something new. He is back to a milder sauce now."

"Hmm," she said. "I guess I'll try it, then."

"If madam is not satisfied, we will offer something else."

"How kind of you."

Laurie handed the waiter the menu without looking at him. Victor was impressed with how the sophisticated Mrs. Prentiss handled herself. He was willing to bet that she would be cool as a cucumber in any situation.

"And you, sir?"

"Beef burgundy, rice, tossed salad with blue cheese." He rattled off his order with machine-gun precision, all the while keeping his eyes on Laurie.

"Very good, sir."

Victor raised his glass to Laurie. "Here's to a pleasant evening," he said.

"I could use one," Laurie muttered as she sipped her wine. Then she quickly apologized. "I'm sorry, Victor. You're kind enough to take me out, and here I am complaining."

He put his hand on hers. "You have nothing to apologize for," he insisted. "That's what friends are for, to lean on when you're weary."

Laurie just sighed and took a healthier sip of her wine.

Victor waited in the silence between them until he could feel the little fist relax beneath his hand.

"Things still tense at home?" he asked solicitously.

She put her glass down and squeezed his hand in both of hers. Her grip was strong and clutching, as if Laurie were groping for a lifeline, fighting a rapid current that was threateningto pull her under. She shook her head several times, staring down at the tablecloth all the while.

"Things should be going just super for Lance and me. After all, I've been acquitted." She shook her head again.

When she looked into his eyes, he almost cringed. There was so much pain and confusion in her face that Victor was taken aback. Gently he coddled her delicate fingers, hoping she could pull strength and comfort from his heart into her own.

"I've been cleared by the law," she repeated. "But now my own husband isn't sure about me."

"Has he accused you of having killed his mother?"

"You know the story?" she asked, but her surprise quickly faded as a cynical frown curved her lips. "What am I saying? Everyone in Genoa City knows the story. I guess that's the disadvantage of living in a small town."

"Given the social prominence of your family and your husband's, everyone would know the story even if you lived in Chicago or New York."

"I guess you're right," she said slowly. "I've become accustomed to the pointing and the stares and the suspicious looks, from strangers anyway. I can tell they're all wondering what really happened. Did Vanessa jump to her death, as I claimed? Or did I push her, as my darling brother-in-law insists?"

"The courts believed you," Victor reminded her. "That should be enough for everyone."

Laurie shrugged. "Everyone knows our court system is fallible. My acquittal could be another example of that. It's not as if a new witness stepped forward and corroborated my story. They just found evidence of Vanessa's illness, which lent credence but not proof to my story. I can still see doubt and worry in people's eyes."

"In Lance's?"

"Yes," she said with a weary sigh. "In

Lance's. Now that the trial's over and life is supposedly returning to normal, I can sense the doubt creeping back into his mind. All during our married life Vanessa tried to break us up, and it looks as if she's going to win with her death.''

Victor didn't know what to say. He'd never been very good at giving comfort, but somehow he sensed that just being there with her was enough. Victor had met Lance at social functions sponsored by members of the business community—luncheons, golf outings, cocktail parties. He appeared to be a good businessman, but he was stupid about his wife. Didn't the man see what a treasure he had in Laurie?

"Oh, phooey," Laurie said, forcing a laugh. "Here comes the salad. Now I have to let go of your hand."

"It'll be here whenever you need it."

Laurie mouthed a thank-you. Her eyes were glistening, and she kept them focused on her plate as she stabbed her fork into a chunk of lettuce.

Midway through her salad, she raised her head. "I'd better start being a pleasant dinner companion or you'll never take me out again."

"You needn't worry," Victor assured her.

She smiled at him, and Victor noticed that the lovely, soft glow had returned to her eyes. She was beautiful, Victor realized, with the same type of classical beauty that Julia had, the type Nikki never could acquire. Laurie was elegant, with an ethereal kind of beauty. Her hair was drawn softly back from her face, highlighting her high cheekbones and the depth of her eyes. Her makeup was unobtrusive. All one saw was the softness of her skin and the long, regal neck that sloped to white shoulders.

Nikki, on the other hand, was earthy. Her eyes glowed with fire, not mystery. She was sensuously attractive, but appealing to the body only, not to the mind. Laurie was pleasure for all the senses.

"Did you enjoy the concert the other night?" Laurie asked.

"I enjoyed the company more," he replied, trying to bring a glow to those cheeks. Her eyes glimmered briefly with pleasure.

"Yes," Laurie said with a laugh. "I would imagine. Two women all to yourself."

His fork stopped midway to his mouth as Victor blinked. Then he remembered that Nikki had been there, too.

"One would have been sufficient," he murmured, looking deeply into her eyes. It was obvious which one he meant, and the blush in her cheeks told him she knew it.

"You're quite a gentleman, Mr. Newman," Laurie said. She leaned back slightly as the waiter removed the salad plates and placed their entrées before them.

"Thank you for your kind words, madam,"

he said. "Whatever I am is but a faint reflection of my companion. I am the moon, you are the sun."

"A woman can wind up feeling very good after a dinner with you."

"It's no less than you deserve," Victor replied.

They addressed themselves to their entrées. The waiter quickly came by to inquire about the sauce. Laurie handled the question with her usual grace, assuring him that it was delicious, but also dismissing him at the same time.

An image of Nikki came briefly to Victor's mind. She probably would have fawned all over the waiter, or embarrassed them all by making a fuss.

Well, that was Nikki. A woman like Laurie would never do anything like that. The world was made up of a lot of peasants and a few queens. And if Lance was too dumb to recognize which he had, then so much the better for Victor. He had always felt an undeniable attraction to queens.

"All the children are asleep," Gwen told the mother superior.

The older nun, who was studying a report, nodded once to acknowledge Gwen's words. Gwen looked up at the clock. It was nine-thirty. Greg would be outside waiting. She wondered if the mother superior had dismissed her or just indicated that she heard.

As if reading her mind, the older woman lifted her pinched face. Sharp brown eyes bored into Gwen's.

"I understand you are going out into the world tonight," the mother superior said.

"Yes, Reverend Mother." The words came out in something of a squeak. Gwen took a deep, calming breath, forcing her vocal cords to relax. "I am meeting with a troubled soul to offer comfort."

The older woman grunted and returned to perusing her report. Gwen hesitated a moment, then decided that she had been dismissed.

"Oh, Sister Magdalene," the mother superior called.

Gwen already had her hand on the doorknob. She turned slightly. "Yes, Reverend Mother?"

"Dispense your comfort frugally. Remember, our Father in heaven wishes that our joy be purely spiritual."

Her lips felt so dry that Gwen was sure they were going to crack. Did the older woman know whom she was going to meet? Did she have special powers from God that allowed her to look deep into a novice's soul?

"Yes, Reverend Mother," Gwen answered.

Gwen received no reply, so she turned and hurried out the door. Beads of sweat appeared on her forehead at her sense of relief at not being questioned further by the mother superior. She really didn't want to enter into a discussion. Gwen herself didn't know why she was meeting Greg. He certainly was a troubled soul; that much was true. But did she intend to leave him only with spiritual joy?

Outside the high walls of the convent, Greg stood next to his car and watched Gwen run across the snow-covered grounds toward him. His heart nearly burst with joy. Gwen's vitality seemed to explode from her body. She ran more like a child than an adult. He wondered if that exuberance came from the hard work and freedom from convention that had filled her childhood days on the farm.

"I'm sorry I'm late," she announced, a trifle breathless.

He stared. Her lips were parted and even in the dim light he could see that her cheeks were flushed. Greg would willingly have stayed there forever, just drinking in her beauty.

"Greg?" She laughed and his heart danced to the music. "Are you mad at me?"

"Never," he said. "I just haven't seen you in a long time. Really seen you, I mean. I could stand here and watch you all night."

She shrugged, somewhat embarrassed by the passion in his voice. "It's just the same old me."

"Thank God for that," Greg murmured. He stepped close to her, but then hesitated. He wanted so badly to take her in his arms, but something prevented him. She wasn't wearing a habit, but her simple clothes looked almost like a uniform. They served as a fence against his feelings. He opened the car door for her and she stepped in.

"Where are we going?" she asked, as he settled into the driver's seat.

"Drinking, dancing, and carousing."

Greg could feel her eyes on him, and he couldn't restrain the smile that burst upon his lips.

She punched him lightly on the shoulder. "Has the legal beagle turned into a comedian since I've seen him last?"

"Not really."

Slowing the car, Greg turned into Center City Park.

Gwen laughed, trying to hide her nervousness. "I don't think parking would be a good idea," she said.

"How about ice-skating?" he asked as he parked.

Her face turned wistful as she looked at the lighted skating area. "When I was a child, we had a little pond out back of the barn," she said. "Poppa was always collecting other people's junk, including old skates, and fixing it up, so we could always skate in the winter."

The bright smile on Gwen's face had all the radiance of a Christmas angel. Greg's troubled soul drank deeply of its peace. She blushed slightly as she noticed him staring at her, then quickly looked back at the skating rink.

"Lots of times the skates didn't match," she

went on. "But they worked just fine, and all of us kids had a lot of fun."

Her last words drifted away, and they sat in silence. Greg could feel his throat grow dry, and the car grew stuffy with tension. Their breath fogged the windows, and he suffered a momentary wish that they would be enclosed in a cocoon, together forever.

"Chris lent us her skates and some thick socks," he said, pulling the gear from the back seat.

"Oh, how nice," Gwen said. She opened her door, swung her feet out, and quickly began to take off her shoes. "It's such a beautiful night; I don't want us to waste a minute of it."

Greg handed her the skates, then went over and sat on a log on the edge of the parking lot to put on his own skates.

Once they were ready, they made their way in silence down to the skating area. Lights and speakers ringed the ice. Earlier the speakers had blared out rock music for the teen set, but now waltzes and fox trots floated in the clear winter air. Greg took Gwen's hand, and they glided out onto the ice.

Both were adequate skaters, and they moved easily across the ice, passing slower couples and avoiding fallen skaters with equal ease. After a short time, though, Greg transferred Gwen's hand to his left hand and slipped his right arm around her waist. She leaned gracefully into him and his heart soared.

There seemed little to talk about, and Gwen turned down his offers of hot dogs and hot chocolate. They skated until perspiration beaded their foreheads; then Greg led her to a bench near one of the many bonfires by the side of the rink.

Gwen took off her gloves and held her hands out to the fire.

"I can warm your hands," Greg told her.

She smiled, but kept her hands to the burningheat as she stared into the flames. "I know," she replied.

Instead of persisting, he leaned back, his arm loosely on her shoulders. There was no reason to rush anything. She was sitting here, comfortably at his side; he didn't need anything else in the world. He sensed the same caution in her that one would see in a doe in the woods. No, he had no intention of pressing her. He didn't want to scare her and send her racing back to the refuge of the convent. If this was the closest he would be able to get to her for a while, then he would savor the moment.

Chapter Eight
Rising Fears

Nikki slammed the door of her little blue Pinto and stood a moment to gaze in admiration at Victor's brown Mercedes coupe as it glimmered in the December afternoon sunshine. When she married Victor, she would have him buy her a red one. She had no intention of choosing some boring color like black or brown.

A flicker of doubt ran through her, but Nikki clenched her jaw and stifled it. He would marry her; he loved her. That was why he'd spent so much time and money changing her. Full of resolution and determination, she marched to the front entrance of his home and rang the bell, smiling at the sound echoing through the heavy wooden door. Nikki liked the chimes; they sounded like church bells. *Real class*, she thought. The door opened and Victor stood frowning at her. "Yes? What are you doing here?" he demanded.

A tremor of uncertainty gave Nikki a brief

shake. Victor had on a sheepskin coat, neatly pressed green slacks, and black cowboy boots. He held a Stetson in his hand, and appeared to be on his way out.

"I thought I'd drop in to see you," she said. Each word was filled with bravado, but Victor stared at her, unmoved.

"You should always call first," he snapped.

"I'm sorry," she said. "I didn't think you had to work today."

"I'm not working. I have a social engagement."

Social engagement? Victor wasn't one for cards with the boys, so Nikki knew it had to involve a female. He was going out on a date. He was going to spend Saturday afternoon with Laurie. The heat of Nikki's anger burned her cheeks, but she restrained herself until it passed.

"As long as it's not anything important, let's chat for a few minutes." She pushed past him and made her way to Victor's den. She threw her coat on the floor and sank back into his leather chair.

"I could use a little something to warm the old bod," she said.

"I don't have much time."

The anger returned, and again Nikki had to force herself to breathe slowly and deeply. Now was not the time to blow up and wreck what could be a very good situation for herself.

"Don't worry about it," she said. "I'm warmingup already."

Victor did not reply. He just stood there and stared at her.

Uncertainty began cooling her again, so Nikki quickly stoked the flames of her courage.

"Okay," she said in a loud voice, gesturing with both hands. "I've decided to darken my hair a bit. It'll still be blond, but a darker blond. You know, so my eyebrows don't show up so bad."

She could see the muscles in his temple tense; Nikki knew that Victor was clenching his teeth. She also saw his eyes slide over to look at the clock on the mantel.

Nikki drew a deep breath. A person needed wind to maintain volume and animation. "So, now we have to make some new outfits. Personally, I like red, as you know, but the designer, she's into blue. So what do you think?"

His eyes went to the clock again.

"I think you should go with pastels," he said. "Light green, blue, yellow, that kind of color."

"Pastels aren't exciting," Nikki complained.

The left side of his lip curled. "Nikki, you've got enough energy in your little finger to excite a platoon of marines."

Tension fled her body, and Nikki slouched down into the chair. "Oh, yeah?" She smiled archly at Victor.

"I wouldn't say it if I didn't mean it." Victor's face turned rock hard again as he looked at his wristwatch. "I hope that's all you have to say, Nikki. I'm late already and I have to go."

His brusqueness swiftly froze her ardor. "Yes. Yes, that's all," she stammered.

He nodded curtly, turning on his heel. At the door he paused. "Sorry, I have to rush. I'll tell Miguel to take care of you." Victor spoke into the intercom in a low voice, instructing Miguel to attend to any of Nikki's requests. Then he was gone without even a glance back.

Nikki's disappointment retreated before the flare of her temper. She stalked to the window and watched Victor's Mercedes turn onto the county road.

That man was hers! He was the best thing she had ever latched on to, and it wasn't only because of his money. Even without his fat wallet, Victor would be a good catch. He was handsome and strong, a super hunk of a man.

Her hands balled up into such tight fists that her nails dug into her palms. Nikki welcomed the pain; it fueled the fires of her anger. Damn that woman, she had a man of her own! What the hell was she doing out prowling? Maybe if she stayed home, her man would come back to her. If she couldn't keep what she had, what the hell made that skinny broad think she could land Victor?

Victor hadn't said anything, but she knew he was going to meet Laurie. There wasn't anyone else. He'd had that forlorn look in his eyes ever since they had met the slender woman at the concert. Nikki shook her head. Victor had the hots for Laurie Prentiss, and for the life of her she couldn't figure out why.

"Madam."

Startled, she spun around. "Who the hell—"

"I'm Miguel, madam." The man made a small bow, then held his small jockylike frame as straight as a rod.

"Yeah?"

"Mr. Newman, madam. He told me to—"

"Oh, yeah." Her eyes narrowed and a broad smile split Nikki's face. "Good to meet you, Miguel."

His bow was deeper this time. "Madam."

"You know the bedroom next to Victor's?"

The man's brow furrowed beneath his thick thatch of white hair. "There's only one bedroom next to Mr. Newman's. It overlooks the paddock, but it's not normally used for guests."

"Yeah, that's the one, Miguel. Fix that one up for me."

His washed-out blue eyes indicated no opinion, but he hesitated.

Nikki batted her long lashes at the little man. "It was Victor's idea."

Miguel bowed slightly. "I understand, madam."

Nikki picked her coat up off the floor. "This came up a bit quickly," she told the houseman. "I've got to run back to my place and get a few things together. I'll be back in an hour."

"Very well, madam."

"Oh, Miguel?"

He turned.

"You got any satin sheets?"

"I believe so, madam."

"Put them on the bed." Nikki smiled. "I'm on the tender side, and Victor doesn't like me to get scratched."

They paused at a fork in the path, and Victor studied the map of the Genoa City Zoo.

"Let's go to the timber wolves exhibit," Victor said.

"Okay." Laurie held on to his arm and squeezed herself up closer to him. It was so nice to be with someone she could relax with, someone whose smile held no hidden questions, no secret accusations. Even being at home and caring for little Brooks hurt these days. Loving the little boy as her own didn't hide the fact that he wasn't hers. He was Lance's and Leslie's child, a further reminder of the troubles in their marriage, a further threat to her peace of mind. But she'd come here with Victor to forget, not to sink deeper into gloom, and she pushed the somber thoughts behind a wall of cheerfulness.

"I thought you were out of your mind when you suggested coming to the zoo," Laurie said with a laugh. "But this is just great —marvelous! I'll never doubt you again, Mr. Newman."

"Thank you, Mrs. Prentiss."

Victor could feel her stiffen, and she pulled slightly away.

"Call me Laurie," she said quietly. "Nothing else."

"I'm sorry." Laurie's troubled relationship

with Lance Prentiss was obviously a touchy subject, and Victor was determined to cheer up his lovely companion today. He looked deep into her stormy eyes; then gallantry moved him. He brought her hand to his lips, gently kissing it.

The corners of her lips twitched, but Laurie kept her smile in place. She was unable to hide the sadness in her eyes, though. They mirrored the pain in her heart. Victor put her arm through his and continued along the path.

"The timber wolves are my favorite exhibit," he said.

"Oh really? That's peculiar." Laurie studied him first from one side and then from the other, trying to see him from a number of angles.

Victor indulged her for a while before he put a scowl on his face. "What are you doing?" he asked with pretended impatience.

"Just verifying a hypothesis."

"Oh?"

Laurie's serious demeanor gave way to hearty laughter. "I detect a strong family resemblance," she claimed.

"Is that right?" he said, forcing a gruffness into his voice. "And in what way do you think I am like a wolf? Am I a lone wolf? A wolf in sheep's clothing?"

"Give me a chance to double-check my theory," she said as they paused to look at the timber wolves relaxing in the snow outside their den. One, obviously the leader, was perched atop a cluster of rocks. A female lay by his side. The other members frisked about in the snow or wrestled with each other.

Turning to face him, Laurie lifted her small gloved hand and stroked his face for a moment. He couldn't quite read her thoughtful expression.

"There *is* a family resemblance . . . somethingin the strength and self-confidence that you exude."

"Anything else?"

"Well." She turned back to the wolves. "You make me feel special, chosen, like that female by the leader's side."

"You are special," Victor said. "You don't need any confirmation from me."

"Sometimes I need a lot of assurance," she said. "A lot."

Sadness and pain were storming her defenses again, threatening to invade her eyes, her mood, her entire being.

"Come on," Victor said, pulling her along before she could become too morose. "Let's go see the seals."

"Victor," she wailed, "it's hard to run in these high-heeled boots."

"Promise to smile and laugh?"

"Yes," she promised.

Finally, he slowed down to a walk. "Good."

She threw her lower lip out in a pout. "You're a big bully, Victor. A big, mean bully."

"Stop pouting," he said. "Or a pigeon will sit on your lip."

"A pigeon." Laurie laughed. "That sounds gross." She shook her head.

Victor looked out of the corner of his eye and saw a little girl's expression of disbelief on her face. He smiled. They would stay at the zoo as long as Laurie wished. They could stay until midnight and he would be able to make her smile and laugh. Smile, laugh, and forget Lance, that weak-minded fool that fate had stupidly dumped on Laurie's shoulders.

Victor drove slowly along his darkened driveway, hesitated a moment at the fork, then proceeded to park in front of his front door. Miguel could put away the Mercedes; he was paid to take care of such things.

"Good evening, sir."

His houseman opened the door as he climbed up the last step. "Good evening, Miguel." Victor let the man take his coat.

"Have a pleasant day, sir?"

"The afternoon was fine," Victor said. "But the evening wasn't anything special. I went to the office and finished up some paperwork."

"The evening is still young, sir."

Victor stared a moment after the houseman. He thought he'd detected a snicker in the man's voice, but the thin, erect figure was already moving down the hall. Shrugging, Victor went up the stairs.

Laurie weighed on his mind. That poor woman should just get rid of Lance. The blasted fool had given her enough cause, with his drinking, gambling, and running away to Paris. Blaming Laurie for his mother's death should have been the last straw. If Prentiss had been any kind of husband, he would have supported her wholeheartedly throughout her courtroom ordeal.

Victor unbuttoned his shirt and pulled it out of his trousers. He would keep in touch with Laurie. It had to be just a matter of time before she sent Lance packing, and when she did, Victor would be there waiting. He flicked the light on and went into his dressing room, throwing his shirt in the laundry hamper, then sitting down to take off his shoes. Once Lance was truly out of the picture, Victor could take over.

Suddenly he stopped in surprise as he glanced into his bedroom. His bed was always neatly turned down by this time, but tonight it looked rumpled. What had his housekeeper done? Victor strode toward the bedroom, but stopped in the doorway, frozen in shock.

"Are you the biggest bear of them all?" Nikki asked. She was lying on her back, smiling up at him. He could see thin strips of black lace over her shoulders, and her smile sizzled with seductiveness.

"What are you doing in my bed?" he asked.

"Oh, yes," she purred, turning over on her side. "You are the biggest bear of them all. Your growl is so deep."

"I asked you what you are doing here."

Victor heard the tremor of anger in his voice, and he could feel his face growing warm. He fought to bring himself under control. Julia had been the last to see him lose his temper, and he was determined that no one else would have that experience.

"The little bed was too small," Nikki said in a little-girl voice. "And the medium bed was too hard." Then, sliding her arm slowly across the sheets in a gesture of obvious invitation, she let her voice drop to a throaty whisper. "But this bed was the biggest and bestest of them all."

She sat up, letting the blanket fall away to reveal a firm, well-rounded body covered by a sheer black-lace nightgown that put a minimum amount of strain on Victor's imagination. The opaque areas of the garment covered approximately two square inches of her flesh. The rest of Nikki's voluptuousness was wrapped in a transparent promise.

What was she doing here? Why was she trying to make him lose control? He would decide when, and if, he made love to her. He was not like the other weak men who'd easily fallen into bed with her.

"Come and join me, sugar," she called.

Rage boiled within him until red spots danced before his eyes. Summoning the discipline that he had cultivated over the past twenty years, he managed to keep his feet riveted to the floor. Victor knew that if he let even a single muscle twitch, he would lose all control. And

Victor Newman never let himself abandon his composure.

"Get out of my room." His voice was a hoarse whisper.

Nikki smiled up at him, and patted the bed. "Victor," she cooed.

He closed his eyes. "Get out of here, right now." He took a deep breath and held it. He would not be a victim of her seductiveness, a victim of his own body's weaknesses. He was in control.

There was a soft rustle, and then he felt her presence brush by him. There was the slightest rustle, so he knew that she'd walked barefoot across his deep plush rug. His body was tight, wound up like a steel spring.

The door slammed, breaking the silence like a blast from a shotgun, and Victor stormed to the window and threw it open. A primeval scream rose in his throat, but he slammed a fist into his mouth before it could escape. He bit his knuckles, drowning the screams that were still trying to fill the room, slamming against his fist like wave after wave of crazed warriors.

Finally, after what seemed like an eternity, Victor managed to focus on the dark night outside. In spite of the cool air, sweat dripped and flowed into his eyes, blurring his vision.

He began to shake violently, but he knew he had won. He had proven himself stronger and better than the other men in her past. He had resisted Nikki's earthy magnetism and had not succumbed. He'd closed his eyes to her soft curves, turned his nose away from the animal-like musk she gave off. He had won.

The tremors ceased, leaving him with only pain: a minor pain in his lacerated knuckles and the excruciating pain of unfulfilled lust everyplace else.

In the room next door, Nikki lay on the bed, puzzled and frustrated. She'd almost had him; she knew it as well as she knew her own name. It was as if she could smell his passion: the heavy scent of his raw, savage desire. She could almost feel Victor ripping at her flesh again and again, until he was completely satiated.

But it was as if some supernatural force had seized Victor and drowned the fires of his passion. Nikki shivered, fear nibbling at the edges of her consciousness. What kind of hold did Laurie Prentiss have on this man?

Chapter Nine

Heaven Found

"How come you always get to sit in the front?" the little boy asked.

"Because I'm bigger than you are," Gwen pointed out. She gave the youngster a fond pat on his cheek before hustling him into the back seat of Greg's car with several other children from the convent's center for abused and abandoned children. A lump rose in Greg's throat, and he had to swallow hard. Gwen would make such a wonderful mother. If only he could be the one to give her children of her own.

"We're ready." She smiled pertly at him.

The lump had not entirely dissolved, so the best Greg could manage was a nod.

Gwen looked at him worriedly as he settled down behind the wheel. "I hope the children weren't too much of a bother."

"Not at all," he said with a smile.

"All children enjoy seeing the Christmas

decorations," she said. "You've been very kind to haul us around."

Greg could feel his ears warm slightly. Driving the children around town had been an excuse to see Gwen, and that's all it was. Hadn't she realized that? "It's no big deal," he mumbled as he pulled the car out into the street.

"It is too a big deal," Gwen scolded. "If it hadn't been for you, none of these children would have been able to see Santa Claus and all the festive-looking store windows."

He stared straight ahead without replying. Gwen was making him out to be a saint, but his feelings toward her were considerably less than saintly.

A while back, in her short skirts and high-heeled boots, Gwen had caused sinful thoughts in ninety percent of Genoa City's male population. Now she did the same thing to him, even though she wore colorless, untailored dresses. When would she see that their love was too strong to deny?

Suddenly she turned around and faced the chattering children in the back seat, a stern look on her face. "Aren't we all forgetting something?"

A chorus of "Thank you, Mr. Foster" quickly followed.

The rest of the ride back to the convent grounds was rather quiet. Even the children's happy voices had wound down to a muted hum. Greg's mind wandered off in a pleasant direction. Gwen would make a wonderful mother, and he would be a good father. He wouldn't run out on his family, as his own father had. No, he would work hard to provide for them, but he would also put aside time to spend with them. He and Gwen would take their children window-shopping during the Christmas season, they would go to the zoo, and in the summer they would go camping. They would have a beautiful family.

"If you're tired, we can skip dinner tonight."

It was as if a blizzard blew a cold wind across his mind. Didn't she want to spend the evening with him?

"No," he insisted. "No, I'm not tired at all."

"Are you sure?" Gwen persisted. "We can just go out for a quick bite after we drop the children off."

"McDonald's. McDonald's." The shouts came from the back seat.

"We're not going to McDonald's," Gwen called back to them. She was trying to imitate a drill sergeant, but she was so far off that even she had to laugh.

"There'll be food for you at the home. Good food," she quickly added to stifle the groans that greeted her words.

Greg waited until the children had settled down, then murmured, "I have most of dinner prepared already. The salad's in the refrigerator, and the roast is in the oven, which the timer should have turned on by now. All I have to do is cook some frozen vegetables."

She shrugged in her cute little way. "Well, it would be a shame to let that food go to waste."

"Indeed it would," he assured her as he pulled to a stop in front of the orphanage.

Greg waited in the car while Gwen escorted the children to their rooms. They'd been out on excursions several times in the past week, and each time Greg saw her, his love grew and grew. He knew that they were meant for each other, that real happiness could only come from sharing their lives. Surely she must know it, too. Why else would she still be seeing him? If she felt nothing for him, she would have said so that first evening. Gwen was gentle and sensitive, but she would know that prolonging their relationship, if she didn't care about him, would only hurt him more in the long run. She hadn't sent him away, though, so Greg was sure that she cared. She had to. . . .

As Greg glanced at his watch, his chilled fingers reminded him how long he'd been waiting for Gwen to come back and join him. Had her superiors rescinded their permission for her to be out this evening? By now they had to be wondering what was going on between them, since he and Gwen had been out several times. He breathed a sigh of relief as she ran into view.

"I was getting a little worried," he said to her when they turned onto the road back to town.

"You were gone a long time. At least it seemed like several years."

Gwen's brow filled with lines of concern. "I'm sorry," she said.

He found her subsequent silence uncomfortable. "I thought your superiors had changed their minds," he blurted out. "You know, about letting you go out with me."

She smiled and shook her head.

"Do they know you're going out with me?"

"I haven't specifically told them who you are," she replied. "But they are aware that you aren't my maiden aunt from Iowa."

"Doesn't that bother them?"

"No," she said. "Most religious orders are much more realistic about these kinds of things now, and this particular order is rather progressive. They don't want me to take my final vows unless I'm really sure I want to stay."

The uncomfortable silence fell around them again, and Greg struck out at it. "What took you so long, then?" he asked. "Were you fooling with your hair or something?"

"Are all attorneys this persistent?" she asked with a forced laugh.

Greg shrugged.

"Actually I went to visit a sick child," she said. "A little boy named Ramón. He's been horribly abused, and he hasn't said a word since he came to the home."

"Oh."

That was typical of Gwen, but for some reason he felt uncomfortable with her explanation. He almost wished she had been fixing her hair or doing something equally inconsequential.

"Here we are," he said, pulling into the parking lot outside his apartment building. He felt a need to dispel the solemn atmosphere that surrounded them, so he spoke in a very hearty manner. "Café Greg. Home of fine dining, dancing, and conversation."

"Sounds wonderful," Gwen said. "I hope it's not expensive."

"Don't worry about it," Greg teased. "I know the owner."

When they got inside, Gwen insisted on helping, so he had her set the table and open the wine. As he moved about, taking care of the last-minute details, he found himself relaxing, the worries ebbing from his soul with each moment. He could feel her presence everywhere. She filled all the empty corners of his apartment, so that he felt her touch no matter where she was.

They still spent most of their days apart, with Gwen at the convent and him at his office, thinking about her, but that was still better than nothing. Someday soon they would reach the point where he could touch her, hold her and love her with his whole heart and soul . . . but that would only happen when she was ready.

Greg knew that they were getting closer and closer to that time. Anybody could see that Gwen wasn't meant to be a nun, but a wife and mother, with children of her own, redheaded little girls like herself.

They sat down to dinner, and Greg let Gwen carry the conversation. She asked him about his work, what cases he was working on, how he was helping people who desperately needed it. Greg answered her questions, but his mind danced ahead to the future, to a time when they would be in their own home, when the empty places at the table would be filled with smiling, freckled faces.

He wanted to love her so much, so very much. Her smiling green eyes flashed at him, and his heart sang: *soon, soon, soon.*

"Good morning." Greg bent to kiss Chris lightly on the cheek. "And how is my beautiful sister-in-law this fine morning?" he asked, breezing by her.

Chris rose from her desk and followed him into his office. He wiggled past stacks of papers and books and flopped into his chair. The broad smile remained on his face as he looked up at her.

"Yes?"

"Yes yourself," Chris said, sitting down in one of his guest chairs. "Are you on something?"

"Why do you ask that? Can't a guy be happy on a Monday morning?"

Chris nodded slowly. "It's a free country," she said. "But when someone who's been moping around for months comes in grinning like a little boy with a chocolate ice cream cone, well . . ." She narrowed her eyes. "Such a big change is just a wee bit hard to cope with."

"That's your problem," he said. "Not mine."

"*Are* you on something?" Chris asked again.

Greg threw his head back and laughed out loud. "I'm high on life."

Chris just stared at him. She was trying to remember what extreme mood changes were symptoms of.

"Good Lord," Greg said in mock exasperation. "There is no pleasing you. First you're on my back for moping, telling me that I depress everyone around me. Now you're telling me I'm too cheerful. What do you want?"

"All I want is for you to be happy."

"I am."

Chris stared at him for another long moment. "Drastic mood swings are not normal," she said.

"Oh-oh." He shrank back in mock terror. "You want to fix me up with another friend. Someone who'll shoot down my enthusiasm and make me morose."

Chris sighed and started to get up. There was no talking to him now.

"Well, don't worry about it," he said. "I have a girlfriend."

Chris sank back into the chair. "Oh, Greg," she almost shrieked. "That's wonderful. Do I know her?"

"Oh, sure. You have for a while. She and I

were close once, and now we're getting back together."

Chris's mouth dropped open, and she ordered her reluctant jaw muscles to shut it. "Nikki?"

"No." His laugh was a warm chuckle. "Gwen and I are back together again."

"Oh, my goodness. She's left the convent?"

He yawned, stretching luxuriantly. "Not yet."

"When is she going to?"

Slight frown lines pulled at his smile. "We haven't really discussed those details yet."

"Oh." Chris didn't know what to say and felt vaguely uncomfortable.

"When am I due in court?" Greg asked.

"You're due in Judge LaRocca's courtroom at ten-thirty this morning. It concerns that class-action suit you brought against the owners of those apartment houses down by the river."

He nodded and rummaged through his brief-case, apparently checking to see that he had everything he needed.

Although Chris stood up, she was reluctant to leave. She remembered her father saying that the highest fliers get hurt the worst when they fall.

"Do the people in charge know that Gwen's seeing you?"

"Convents are much more liberal these days," Greg said, "especially the one that Gwen joined."

"I know that," she said with a giggle. "But I don't think nuns are allowed to have boyfriends."

"I told you," he snapped, "it's a very modern order. Anyway Gwen's going to leave the convent. She's not really a nun yet, so she can leave any time she wants to."

Then why hadn't she? Chris wondered. Was she just playing a game with Greg? No, more than likely she just couldn't make up her mind what she wanted to do. Or maybe she was suffering from last-minute jitters. That was understandable, but Greg was the one who was going to get hurt if she was just toying with his emotions until she could make up her mind.

"It sounds like you and Gwen have only gone out once or twice."

"Yes, but we know each other very well."

His smile had definitely vanished. Obviously the subject was a sensitive one with her brother-in-law. Chris forced herself to proceed slowly.

"I know that," Chris said. "All I meant is that it sounds as if you and Gwen are just friends. Neither of you has made a commitment to the other."

He frowned at her.

"I don't mean to imply that there is anything wrong with that," she said. "I don't see any reason why a man and a woman can't be friends. I think people carry the sexual attraction too far."

"There are other attractions besides sex," he

said. "Love is the most powerful attraction of all."

Chris wondered how Gwen felt. The beautiful redhead had walked out on Greg once before. What was she up to now?

"If you don't have any further questions, please excuse me," Greg said. "I need to review these briefs before my meeting with Judge LaRocca."

"Okay," she said. "I have some stuff to catch up on myself."

Chris forced herself not to look back at Greg as she left him to his work. She merely hoped that he wouldn't be hurt again.

"Hey, Vic," the Bayou's bartender greeted him. "You want your usual?"

Victor did not acknowledge that he had heard him. "Martini, please," he ordered. "Extra dry."

He didn't really like martinis, but he hated it when people tried to get familiar with him, and the martini was the first drink that had come to mind.

The bartender returned with his drink, and Victor placed a crisp bill on the bar.

"That's okay, Vic. I'll just run a tab for you. Pay when you leave, like you usually do."

"I don't expect to have another."

Victor hoped that the coldness in his voice would put the man off, but apparently the signals had gone right over his head.

The bartender leaned on one elbow, looked

up at the stage, and snickered. "She sure can shake it," he mumbled.

Even as his irritation grew, Victor had to admit that the bartender was right. Many women didn't mind taking off their clothes, but they had no spirit or talent, so they just moved about clumsily. Nikki liked to show off, and she had all the necessary skills and energy to present herself well. Her act was a bit on the raunchy side, but she obviously enjoyed herself. When it came to stripping, Nikki was a true professional.

She caught sight of Victor and blew him a kiss. The Bayou regulars cast him a quick glance, then turned their attention back to Nikki. Victor clenched his teeth. He would either have to get her out of this joint or quit coming by. Everyone and his brother now regarded him and Nikki as an item. He was back to the issue of control again, and around here, Nikki was judged to be winning.

"How do the customers like the changes in Nikki's routine?" Victor asked.

The bartender shrugged. "Skin is skin. Hell, Vic. These farmers don't notice what Nikki's wearing or what kind of routine she goes through. All they see is that body and all those curves and they start drooling and panting."

Victor didn't respond. The man was right. The typical low-life Bayou customer wouldn't recognize talent if it bit him on the leg. If Nikki were going to progress, he would have to get her out of here. He would have to start looking into some Chicago bookings. It would put her farther away, where he couldn't keep a close eye on her, but maybe that would be best. Farther away, her body wouldn't tempt him so. But he probably should find her a good road manager first.

"Hey, Vic." The bartender barged into his thoughts. "Why don't you build Nikki a stage at your place so she can dance for you in private? I hear you can afford it."

Victor ignored the rube. Had Nikki been bragging again? But that really wasn't like her, and anyway, in a small town like Genoa City many people would know he was well off.

"Or do you get your jollies from having other guys watch your woman?" the bartender asked.

This time Victor fixed the bartender with a hard stare. It was obvious that the man had spent so much time among the Bayou's vulgar clientele that he had turned into a slug. With a snort, Victor turned from the bar. Nikki was about through with her act. He would wait for her in her dressing room.

"Hey, Vic," the bartender called. "What do you want me to do with your drink?"

Victor didn't bother to answer.

From her perch on the stage Nikki had been watching Victor. That scene at his house the other night had confused her, but regardless of what he'd done—or not done—he still kept coming around to see her dance. That proved he liked her, didn't it? She put some extra twists and turns and verve in her finale, then jumped off the stage and ran for the dressing rooms with a teasing laugh for her audience. The boys out front were about to tear the joint down.

"Hi, honey," she bubbled when she found Victor waiting for her in the hallway.

He returned her greeting with a dark look as she led him inside the dressing room, but that didn't bother Nikki. She knew he was shy and didn't like to show his feelings with all the other dancers and waitresses hanging around and gawking.

"Hear that?" she asked, gesturing toward the bar. "If they cheer any louder, the roof will come down. I'm the best, right?"

Victor's face was a blank slate, void of interest or emotion. "You're coming along quite well," he said after a short pause. "I'll ask Madame Sonja to make some additional changes in your dance routine. Then we should look into moving on."

Victor spoke in such a low voice that Nikki had to strain to hear him. He liked private conversations, but it wasn't easy to talk privately in the large communal dressing room shared by all of the female employees at the Bayou. Nikki knew it was one of the reasons Victor didn't come to the dressing room all that often.

"Sure, Victor," she said. Moving on to what? she wondered. Did he mean getting married?

"I'll call you when I have things organized," he said.

"Sure, babe." She moved forward to kiss him, but he thrust his forearm against her rib cage and pushed her away. Then, without another word, he quickly marched out.

Nikki quivered as a collection of emotions churned within her to form a stew of bitterness, but she kept a wide smile on her lips. For a good part of her life, pride had been her only possession, and she wasn't going to give it up now.

"I tell you," she said to no one in particular, examining her shiny blond hair in the mirror. "A big executive type and he's as shy as a kid who grew up in the woods."

Murmurs and chuckles answered her.

"He doesn't show much emotion in public," Nikki went on, flinging her feather boa onto a dressing table. "But once the shades are pulled and the lights are out, bar the door! I get more loving in one hour than all the married women in Genoa City get in a month of Sundays."

Her co-workers whooped and hollered while Nikki demonstrated a little bump and grind.

"It's still early," Nikki said, looking at the wall clock. "Looks like I got enough time to grab a few brews before my next act."

She sauntered out to the bar. Men leered at her, and the braver ones shouted suggestions, but she ignored them all. It had been several weeks since Victor first came to the club to talk to her and offer to help her with her act, yet nothing had happened between them. No man had held out on her that long before. It couldn't be that skinny little Laurie was serving his needs, could it? No, there had to be something else standing in the way. Nikki licked her lips, determined and intrigued. She would snag Victor Newman—come hell or high water!

Chapter Ten
Questions

Gwen saw Greg's car slow down just before it reached the little dip in the drive that would hide it behind the clump of evergreens. Even though she couldn't see him from her perch on the front steps of the convent, she knew that he was waving good-bye to her. She waved back, the car moved on, and she could see only an occasional flash of blue among the trees. Soon even that was gone, and Gwen knew he was on the road to home.

She sighed as she stood up and turned toward the entrance. That same home could be hers, filled with a loving husband and, God willing, children of their own.

She paused, her hand on the doorknob, struck by her own thoughts. *God willing.* What was God's will? What did he want her to do with her life? She had been eager to devote herself to his work, but now doubts filled her.

Where had those doubts come from? Did they come from her attachment to worldly things?

Then an almost painful thought came to her and she turned away from the door. Had the doubts come from God himself? Perhaps this confusion was his way of telling her that she wasn't worthy of serving him. Maybe God was trying to give her a message that, with her history, she could never be his servant.

"Oh, Lord, what do you want?" she asked the afternoon sky. But the sparse clouds held no answer.

Why had Greg reentered her life? But just as quickly as that thought crossed her mind, she was filled with guilt. She had no right to blame Greg. She had a free will, and Greg had a right to his share of happiness in this world. If she really didn't want him, she shouldn't have encouraged him. No one had made her go on a date with him.

A date. She winced at the thought, but there was no denying it. She had gone on a date with Greg, and not just once.

Her shoulders slumped. She didn't know what to do. She was so deep in thought that her steps took her away from the convent and led her down the path to the chapel. There was a small oratory in the convent itself, but it was usually occupied by nuns. She needed to be alone, alone with God.

Gwen tiptoed up the steps and opened the chapel door a crack. The only light in the dark interior came from the banks of votive candles flickering at the foot of the altar. She opened the door wider and took a closer look around the church, wanting to make sure that no one else was present. The chapel appeared empty, and she went in.

Sliding into the last pew, Gwen fell to her knees, dropping her head to her folded hands. For the umpteenth time she asked God for forgiveness. Although she knew that what she had done in the past was wrong, she did not plead extenuating circumstances. She just said she was sorry for her previous life of drugs and prostitution and asked God for mercy and forgiveness.

She knew that Greg wanted her. But did God want her? And did she want to dedicate her life to God? Or was she searching for a way to pay for her life of sin? Was that why she had come to the convent?

Sitting back in the pew, Gwen felt more tired and lost than when she had come into the chapel. She needed a sign. She needed God to tell her directly whether he wanted her or not. If he didn't, she would give herself to Greg.

But the chapel remained dark and silent. Gwen saw no signs, heard no answers, received no guidance. There was only silence.

Laurie had just laid Brooks down for his nap when the doorbell rang. Her heart fluttered a bit as she hurried to the front door. Maybe it was Lance. Maybe he had decided to take off from work early, to spend some time with her.

Hope brought a blush of color her face. No matter what had happened, she still loved Lance. If only they could work things out . . .

But it wasn't Lance at the door; it was a young blond woman. "I was hoping you'd be home," the young woman said as she pushed past Laurie.

"I beg your pardon?" Laurie protested, then paused. The woman looked somewhat familiar.

"We have to talk," the woman said. "Where do you want to do it?"

"Don't I know you from somewhere?"

"Yeah," the woman said, sauntering in. She peered into the rooms near the entryway and then pointed to the den. "This looks good. Let's have our little chat in here."

"Who are you?" Laurie asked.

"Nikki." She went into the den, and Laurie followed her, remembering where she had seen the woman before.

"You were with Victor Newman at the concert the other night, weren't you?" Laurie asked.

Nikki settled down on the sofa, propping her feet up on the cushions. "Yeah," she said. "Victor and I were out on the town when you pushed your way in."

It all came back. Victor had introduced her as Nikki Reed. Later Laurie remembered that the woman had been married to Greg Foster for a while. She was a stripper and had been involved in some kind of scandal involving the death of her father. Greg had defended her and had gotten her off.

"You were married to Greg Foster," Laurie said. "Weren't you?"

"Yeah."

"His brother is married to my sister."

"Small world. But that's neither here nor there," Nikki said. "I came here to talk about you and Victor. Sit down."

Laurie's mouth opened in shock. Who did this woman think she was, barging into her home and ordering her about?

As if reading her mind, Nikki laughed. "You'd better get some help if you're thinking about throwing me out. You don't look nearly strong enough."

The only other person in the house was little Brooks! Laurie swallowed back a wave of panic and sat down in a chair. "What is it you wish to speak about?" she asked, trying to keep her voice cool.

"We aren't going to have a conversation, lady," Nikki snapped. "I'm just here to warn you: keep your paws off Victor. I had my claim staked before you even came along."

Laurie was stunned at the suggestion that she was after Victor. "I'm a married woman," she said. "I have no intention of chasing any man around."

"I know you're married. That doesn't matter. I want to know why you're messing around with Victor."

"I've been having some personal problems, and he's a friend." Laurie bit her lip. Her fury at the woman pushing into her home was mixed with the shame of admitting that her marriage was on shaky grounds. "Victor was nice enough to comfort me when I needed it."

"Is that right?"

The woman's sneering, twisted smile was like a window into her filthy mind. "It's not what you think," Laurie insisted, anger warming her cheeks even though she realized she shouldn't lower herself to answer this woman's accusations. "Victor was just offering his sympathy."

"Good." Nikki laughed. "Because I'm woman enough to provide all the loving Victor will ever need. So you just concentrate on your husband. And if you can't get his fire lit, then go find somebody else. Victor's mine."

Laurie stared dumbfounded at the woman. *Do I look like the type who chases after men?* she wondered. Her lips squeezed into a thin line. Well, she might have done something like that years ago, but all young women did. She was a married woman now, a wife and mother.

"I am not pursuing Victor or anybody else, and I have no plans to do so," Laurie said coldly.

Nikki rose from the sofa and paused, resting her hands on her hips. "Good," she proclaimed. "Because if I even get a hint of you making eyes at Victor, I'm going to visit you again. And we won't have another civil conversation. I can guarantee you, we'll have a good old-fashioned knock-down drag-out.''

Although Laurie was disarmed, she refused to look away from the woman's intent gaze.

''Do you understand?''

Laurie nodded, blinking at the menacing tone in the woman's voice.

''Don't get up,'' Nikki said. ''I can find my way out. Oh, hey,'' she called from the door, ''good luck with your husband.''

The slamming of the front door signaled Nikki's departure, but Laurie just sat and stared into space. What in the world was happening to her life? Her husband was rarely home, and a strange woman was accusing her of chasing after her man. This all had to be a bad dream. Soon she would wake up and Lance would love her again.

No, Laurie thought with a sigh as she got to her feet, there would be no waking up. Lance didn't love her as he once had, and his heart no longer belonged to her. He was spending more time at work and less at home, and he was getting closer to his brother Lucas. For a time, the brothers had avoided each other, since it had been Lucas's testimony that had put Laurie in prison.

Troubled, Laurie rose and checked on Brooks. Seeing that he was sleeping peacefully, she went out on the balcony, the same balcony that Vanessa had leaped from. A cold winter's wind blew from the northwest, cutting through the bulky wool sweater she wore. Laurie shivered and hugged herself, but she didn't go back inside.

Through all her troubles, it had been Victor, not Lance, who had comforted her. In fact, Lance had been the cause of a good part of her problems, while Victor had been kind, gentle, and caring. He treated her like a lady, taking her out and, most of the time, just listening to her. The little he did say was usually to make her laugh.

Victor was a charitable man. In this Christmas season he was offering her peace and goodwill. And that was all. But now, because of this kind man, she was the object of threats from a strange woman. Laurie shivered again, and the chill was from more than the cold. That blond woman was so menacing. With her broad shoulders and voluptuous body, men would consider her sexy, but Laurie had sensed the muscles beneath those curves. That woman could do her harm.

The ringing of the telephone called for her attention, and Laurie hurried into the house to answer it before it awoke Brooks.

"Hello."

It was Lance, his voice flat and businesslike. "Laurie, I'm going to have to work late today, so I won't make it home for dinner."

"I'm sorry to hear that, dear," Laurie said softly, desperate to dispel her disturbing thoughts. "I'll leave something in the oven for—"

"Don't bother," Lance interrupted her coldly. "I really don't know what time I'll be home. I can always grab a bite somewhere."

"Lance, I—"

This time the dial tone interrupted her, and Laurie hung up the phone slowly. He probably didn't want to hear her tell him that she loved him anyway.

Laurie turned and stared out the window. She was losing her husband. And now that woman wanted to deny her the comfort of a sympathetic friend. Vanessa's act of vengeance was taking its toll. Would Laurie ever find peace?

"Yeah?" Nikki shouted into the phone.

She felt slightly dizzy after popping up in bed to answer the telephone. Whoever was calling had better have a damn good reason or hope that she didn't know him.

"Nikki?"

"What do you want?"

"Hey, ease up."

The male voice was vaguely familiar, and that added to the turmoil in Nikki's head. She rubbed her eyes and lay back down on the bed.

"Did I get you up? What were you doing, partying until morning?"

"No, you jerk," she mumbled. "I work until morning. The Bayou doesn't close until four in the A.M."

"Hey, sorry about that, Nikki," the caller cheerfully replied. "This is Cat, Cat Nolan."

The private detective she'd hired. Suddenly awake, Nikki sat up in bed.

"Oh, yeah, Cat," she said. "I didn't recognize your voice." She pushed a pair of shoes off the bed and onto the floor. The bedside clock she uncovered showed nine-fifteen. "It's still the middle of the night for me."

"Sorry, Nikki."

She forced her eyes open wide and twisted her head, stretching her neck muscles.

"So what do you want?" she asked. "It's your nickel."

"Not hardly," he said with a raspy chuckle. "Everything I do for you is on your tab."

Nikki was now wide awake, with a fully functioning brain. "All right," she snapped. "Then quit dinking around. You got something to say, spit it out."

"I got a lot, believe me. Three bags full."

"All right, all right already. So give it to me."

"I got Victor Newman's life story all wrapped up," Cat Nolan told her. "I'll have it typed up later on, and I'll mail it out to you."

"Give it to me now," Nikki said. "Over the phone."

"I told you I got a lot," he said. "What do you think three bags full means?"

"All right, give me bits and pieces. You know, like highlights, coming attractions."

Cat started chuckling, which apparently aggravated his lungs, and he began to cough. Finally composing himself, he continued.

"Okay, let me start at the beginning," he said. "Victor was born in Germany."

"Sometimes he talks like a foreigner," Nikki said. "Has he got a family there?"

"I can't vouch for his speech pattern," Cat Nolan replied. "But he doesn't have any family anywhere. He was raised in an orphanage. Not one of the better institutions, either."

Nikki grunted.

Cat then went on a rambling journey through his notes. His phrases were punctuated with coughing and mumbling, but from his words Nikki was able to draw the sharpest picture she had ever had of Victor Newman. Born in extreme poverty, orphaned at a young age, he'd fought and scraped for everything he had. He'd gone to night school, worked harder than anyone else, conquered one set of problems and then moved on to the next opportunity. Always running, he'd struggled to flee the deprivation and poverty that he could not erase from his soul.

Nikki was smiling as Cat's narrative drew to a close. This little call from Chicago would turn out to be cheap at twice the price, three or four times even. For the first time she knew exactly who Victor Newman was. Now she knew how to get to him.

"That's about it." Cat's voice interrupted her daydreaming, and Nikki snapped to attention. "You still want the report?"

"If I'm paying for it, I want it." Nikki

slammed the receiver down, but her face was wreathed in a smile.

Men like Victor never really had a childhood. So deep down they were little boys all their lives. Nikki's eyes misted over. *Poor little feller!* she thought. He'd probably never had any kind of Christmas in his life. Santa Claus had probably never visited him.

Nikki snuggled back down under the covers. Victor wouldn't need Santa Claus. She would make up for all the Christmas mornings he had missed.

Chapter Eleven

Beginnings and Endings

The grass felt soft beneath Gwen's bare feet, and a warm breeze caressed her legs beneath her billowing dress. Greg held her hand as they walked purposefully toward the old barn on the horizon. Gwen was titillated, filled with need and desire.

Unable to wait, she started running toward the barn. Greg followed her, and soon they were running, running, running, but they couldn't get any closer. The barn kept receding, moved into the distance horizon. Gwen cried out in the anguish of her unfulfilled desire.

Suddenly the world turned dark and cold, and Gwen sat up. Her nightgown was damp with perspiration, and she was shivering from the wet chill. Climbing out of bed, she pulled on her robe and walked to the window, the bare floor cold beneath her feet. Outside the world was cold and dark, with the look of desolation common to a Wisconsin winter at four in the morning.

Gwen shivered again, but it was more from the memory of the dream than from the cold of her bare room. She was frightened and confused. She hadn't dreamed of Greg in a long time, especially not in that kind of erotic imagery, but what was worse was the feeling that remained with her. Never since she'd entered the convent had she awakened with her flesh so hungry for the touch of a man. If Greg were here right now in her chilly, simply decorated room she would willingly let him take her. Her body shook again with the ache of desire. No, she would demand that he take her.

Letting the curtain fall, Gwen turned sadly from the winter scene and went to sit in her chair. The straight-backed wooden chair was uncomfortable, but Gwen saw no reason to return to bed. She would be getting up in another hour or so anyway for morning prayers and breakfast.

She leaned back and closed her eyes, letting the frigid air of the room cool her fevered body. If the truth be known, Gwen was afraid to go back to bed, afraid she would fall asleep and return to the sensual dreams of her sinful flesh.

Choking back the lump in her throat, Gwen sighed. She'd asked for a sign, and God had sent her one. He did not want her—at least not as a nun. She was incapable of a life of religious service.

When the bells rang for morning prayers, Gwen got up from the chair to dress. Sadness hung over her like the sackcloth of a penitent sinner. She scolded herself, telling herself that she was fortunate to have the love of a man like Greg. Some women who left the convent had no one to go to. Gwen dressed quickly. She wanted to speak to the mother superior before prayers.

She hurried down the stairs, then breathed a sigh of relief when she reached the bottom. The mother superior, as usual, was pacing in front of the door to the oratory.

"Reverend Mother," Gwen said, "may I speak with you, please?"

The older nun stopped her pacing. "Certainly, Sister Magdalene."

Suddenly Gwen felt tongue-tied. "I don't know how to begin," she said.

"You have doubts about your vocation."

"Yes." Gwen hung her head in shame.

"That is not unusual, child," the mother superior gently assured her. "Most of us live with doubt for a good part of our lives."

"I am not worthy to serve God," Gwen said.

"None of us are," the nun said. "But God does not mind." Then for the first time since they'd met, Gwen saw the mother superior smile. "He really has no choice, child. Unfortunately we are the best he has to work with."

Gwen felt even more ashamed. The nun thought her doubts were due to her humility.

"There's a man, Reverend Mother." She had to explain before the mother superior clothed her in sainthood.

"There are many men," she replied.

"There is one that I am very attracted to," Gwen went on to explain. She tried to look the mother superior in the eye, but couldn't.

"That is not unusual, Sister. God meant that to be."

"But he is very attractive to me."

"I assure you. That is not unusual."

Something in the woman's tired voice made Gwen look up. But the face was as pinched as always, and the normal sternness in the eyes had not diminished.

There was the sound of footsteps on the stairs, and the mother superior's voice grew softer. "We all have doubts, Sister Magdalene. Believe me. They will live with you all of your life."

Gwen opened her mouth to speak. She wanted to explain that it wasn't just doubts. "I asked God for a sign," Gwen said. "And he spoke. He does not want me."

The woman smiled again, but this time her smile was cynical. "He came to your room and spoke directly to you?"

"No," Gwen replied. "It was . . . it was in a dream."

The nun studied a spot on the wall beyond Gwen's head. "We do not come here because we do not love man," she said slowly. "We come because we love God more."

Gwen stayed silent, not knowing how to reply.

Three sisters came down the stairs and made their way into the oratory. "God's signs are not easy to read," the mother superior said. "They require all of our attention and a great deal of contemplation."

"I know," Gwen answered. "But—"

"Think on it, Sister Magdalene." The mother superior's voice took on its usual commanding tone. She nodded toward the oratory. "This is a good place to start."

Gwen blessed herself at the holy water font and started to follow the other sisters into the oratory, but then she hesitated. Contemplation would do no good. God had already rejected her. Her sinful flesh would never allow her to serve him properly. Of that she was absolutely sure.

She turned aside, hurrying down the hallway to a phone. Her shaking fingers dialed a number, and she waited, unable to breathe, until she heard Greg's voice.

"Greg," she said softly, tears forming in her eyes at the gentleness in his voice. "Greg, I've made a decision. I'm leaving. Will you come and take me home?"

"Need any help?" Nikki asked.

Victor didn't look up from the report he was reviewing. "I have all the help I need," he replied. "Miguel always packs for my trips. He knows exactly what I need."

Nikki kicked off her shoes and curled her feet under her. She glanced at Victor's stern mask and smiled to herself. Miguel didn't know what he needed; she did. After learning about his childhood, Nikki was sure that she was the only one who knew exactly what Victor needed.

She looked thoughtfully around the room. It was hard to decide where to put the Christmas tree in Victor's house. The obvious place was the living room with its eighteen-foot ceiling. She could put an enormous tree in there. But this den was obviously Victor's favorite room. He spent most of his time here, and this was the room he always brought her to.

A broad smile lit Nikki's face. Of course, why hadn't she thought of it before? She would get two Christmas trees: a large one for the living room and a small one for the den.

"I really appreciate you letting me stay here while they're redecorating my apartment," she said.

"No problem," Victor replied distractedly. "I'll be gone for a few days."

After a moment he looked up. "And even if I were here it would be no problem," he said without a smile. "The house is big enough so that we wouldn't interfere with each other."

He turned his attention back to the report, and Nikki studied him. Poor Victor. He'd been hurt so many times that he was afraid to let people get close to him. During a second phone call, the private detective had told her about Julia.

"Sir." They both looked up at Miguel. "The limousine is here to take you to the airport."

Victor rose and stuffed the report in his briefcase. He walked out without a word.

Nikki rushed to the window and watched him walk to the limousine. She would have liked to kiss him and tell him to take care of himself. She wanted him to know that he would have somebody warm and loving to come home to, but she knew better than to push Victor. She gave a small wave as the car rounded the curve in the driveway.

Once the car had disappeared from sight, Nikki marched resolutely into the den. Pressingthe intercom button, she barked into it, "Miguel, would you and Helga come into the den, please?"

Without bothering to wait for a reply, Nikki settled into the big chair behind Victor's desk. She smiled to herself. Victor would be proud of her. She was really getting the hang of running a place like this.

Victor's houseman and housekeeper stepped tentatively into the den.

"Come in," Nikki called in her usual hearty manner. "Sit down. I have a few things I want to cover."

Miguel and the housekeeper looked at each other curiously, but they obeyed her command.

Full of joyous excitement, Nikki leaned forward and rested her elbows on the desk. "The three of us are going to turn this place into something special," she said. "We're going to decorate this house for Christmas, inside and out."

Helga's face registered no emotion, but Miguel frowned in concern.

"Don't worry," Nikki hastened to assure them. "I'm not planning for us to do it by ourselves. I've lined up a bunch of folks from town. They'll be out here in about thirty minutes."

"I wasn't worried about the work." Miguel hesitated a moment. "I was more concerned about Mr. Newman's reaction. This house has never been decorated before—for anything."

"I know," Nikki said. "It's going to be a surprise."

Miguel shook his head. "I'm not sure that's wise, madam."

"Oh, Miguel." Helga laid a hand on his arm. "Just think, Christmas decorations! We haven't had them for so long. I miss them terribly."

Miguel shook his head again but said nothing.

"What do you want us to do, miss?" Helga asked, her voice giddy with excitement. Her eyes shone like a little girl's, and Nikki felt her own eyes misting.

"We're going to have a lot of people out here," she said. "I just want the three of us to keep them full of coffee and make sure they don't steal anything."

Helga laughed, but Miguel's face remained solemn as Nikki sent them off to make coffee. Fortunately the tradesmen arrived before Miguel's concern could grow into full-blown doubt.

The rest of the afternoon and into the eveningNikki had little time for worry. She was racing all over the mansion, inside and outside. She went along with the tradesmen's suggestions for most things, because she was concerned that her own tastes would be too garish for Victor. But she did send them back three times to get a bigger tree for the living room. There was some grumbling, but Nikki could outswear a stevedore, and the men soon fell into line.

When the last of them packed up and left around ten in the evening, Nikki ventured outside to inspect the house with Helga and Miguel. The stableman joined them. All agreed that the mansion looked magnificent.

As they walked in the front door, they found the tree in the high-ceilinged living room overwhelmingly beautiful. Helga, teary-eyed, kissed Nikki on both cheeks. She whispered that the house was just lovely, like the old houses she'd worked in back home in Bavaria.

Nikki went upstairs, tired but happy. She put on her neglige, brushed her teeth, and then went into Victor's room. As she sat on the bed, plumping up his pillow, her stomach quivered with excitement. Nikki could hardly wait for Victor to come home. She wanted to see his face when he saw what they had done. He would tell her that he loved her then; she just knew it.

"Take it easy, Mr. Foster. This road isn't for fast driving, especially not with all the snow we've had lately."

"I'm sorry, Officer," Greg said. "And thanks."

Breathing a sigh of relief, Greg pulled his car back on the road. He'd been clocked at twenty-five miles over the speed limit. That policeman could have thrown the book at him, given the slick road conditions. He was lucky that he knew the guy from court. He was especially lucky, since he was primarily a defense lawyer, that the man remembered him in a positive light and let him off.

"Oh, boy," Greg muttered. He was doing it again. Touching the brakes lightly, he slowed his car down to the speed limit. If that officer caught him again, he would really be in hot water.

"Damn," he shouted, pounding the steering wheel. "I wish I could fly." If he could fly he would arrive at that convent in half a second, even less.

As he stopped for a red light, his body trembled with anticipation. He needed to control himself until he had Gwen out of the convent and safely in his arms. Greg remembered an old saying about the higher you were the farther you fell . . . and the more it hurt.

The light turned green and his tires squealed in protest as he floored the accelerator. He wasn't going to fall this time. He and Gwen had had many discussions, and she had said that she needed time to think things over. Well, she had taken the time, and she had chosen him.

A lump rose in his throat, and the road blurred as his eyes misted. At last he was going to have the one person he really loved. He could see that now. All the others had either been crushes or merely physical attractions. Gwen was the one he truly loved, the one he wanted to spend the rest of his life with. He wanted to have children with her. He wanted to grow old with her and spend their days in the sunset, pasting pictures of their grandchildren in the family scrapbook.

Although it took an enormous act of will, Greg stayed within the speed limit the rest of the way to the convent. Half a lifetime later the old brick and stone buildings appeared on the horizon. His hands shook, and he had to bite his lip to keep the tears inside. He couldn't believe that God would want such a loving woman as Gwen to go through life without a family, and God had shown that he agreed. "Thank you, God," he murmured. "Thank you for bringing Gwen back into my empty life."

Greg turned into the grounds and drove slowly toward the convent. "What in the world?" he mouthed in the silence of his car.

A child was teetering on top of the stone wall

along the drive. Greg slowed to a crawl. What was the kid doing?

"Oh, no!"

The child suddenly pitched forward and fell to the ground. Greg stopped his car and ran over to the thin body, now lying so still at the base of the stone wall. The child's head was cut and swelling where he had apparently struck some stones on the ground. Greg gently picked the boy up and put him in the car. Then he drove quickly to the main building.

Holding the boy in his arms, Greg rang the doorbell. When it wasn't opened right away, he started kicking at the thick oaken door. The child lay motionless in his arms.

"Hurry up," he shouted. "Damn it, hurry up."

The door flew open, and an old woman glared at him. She was dressed in the simple clothes of a servant of God, but she wore the face of a warrior queen.

"Sir, what is the meaning of—"

"He's hurt." Greg spat the words out. "He fell from the top of the—"

The woman snapped out orders like a general on the battlefield. "Bring him in."

She pointed to a couch. "Put him there."

Before the words were out she was ringing a bell. Running footsteps answered.

"It's Ramón," a voice exclaimed.

"Ice. Bandages." The commands came, crackling like rifle fire.

Greg found himself pushed aside by the whirl of activity surrounding the child. He stood in the puddle formed by the snow melting off his shoes.

The boy's cut was cleaned, and ice was applied to the bump. Soon his eyes began to flutter. He groaned. Then his lips moved and a murmur floated up.

A young sister gasped. "Is he speaking?" A hush settled over the room.

"Sister Magdalene?" the boy mumbled.

Another sister clasped her hands to her mouth and then made the sign of the cross.

"Get Sister Magdalene," the warrior queen barked. "Bring her here immediately."

"Sister Magdalene." The boy spoke the nun's name again, then his voice grew stronger and louder. "Sister Magdalene," he called.

Quick steps answered the boy's call. Greg looked up to see Gwen hurrying down the hallway. He moved toward her, but she brushed right by him. Greg stared as she cradled the child in her arms.

The boy started crying and laid his head on Gwen's breast as she hugged him.

Her eyes glistened as she brushed his hair back and assured him everything would be fine now. Picking up the skinny little boy in her arms, she turned to carry him down the hallway.

"Gwen?" Greg called, hurt that she hadn't even acknowledged his presence.

"Later," she whispered.

Later. How many lifetimes later? Greg wondered. He plodded into the waiting room and slumped down into a chair. *Later*, his own Gwen had told him. A cold fear seized his heart as he looked down from the heights he'd traveled this morning. It was such a long way to fall. Gritting his teeth, Greg opened his eyes and forced himself to focus on a picture that hung on the wall, a painting of a woman with her bare heel on the neck of a snake. He wasn't going to fall. Gwen would see that the child was taken care of, and then she would come to him.

"Mr. Foster?"

He turned to stare into the intense eyes of the warrior queen.

"I'm Sister Julian," she said, holding out her hand. "I am the mother superior at this convent."

Greg rose and shook her hand. "Can I see Gwen?" he asked.

The woman nodded. "Sister Magdalene is taking care of Ramón. She'll soon be free."

He nodded and looked nervously around at the spare little room.

"Ramón has suffered more in his few years than most of us do in a lifetime. He was abused by his own mother. It so shocked him that he has not spoken since he came here. We were sure his silence wasn't a physical problem, so we are all quite excited today. His speaking is a major breakthrough."

"Yes," Greg murmured. "I can understand that."

"Sister Magdalene has made him her personal project," the nun said quietly. "She has a special empathy for the abused children who come here."

Greg could only nod. He was peering over the edge of a chasm again, and fear froze his vocal cords.

"Here is Sister Magdalene now."

The woman quietly left, and he and Gwen were alone. The cold icy fear had spread throughout his entire body.

Gwen had no bags with her, but Greg took her by the arm. "Let's go," he said.

"Greg," she said in an almost whisper. "Sit down."

Although he was still overcome with cold, a sweat broke out on his body.

"Gwen." His voice revealed his raw emotion. "Let's go, right now."

She stared at him for a long moment. Greg felt himself teetering on the edge.

"I'm sorry," she said softly.

He fell. His throat ached to cry out in fear and pain. "Gwen."

"This is where I belong."

He kept falling, falling, falling so far down. He wanted so badly to scream. "Please, Gwen," he whispered.

Her eyes were shiny with tears as she shook her head. "I've been praying so hard," she told him. "I've pleaded with God to give me a sign to tell me where he wants me—here or out in the world."

"Please, Gwen. *I* want you, I need you, so much."

"He answered me today. God needs me here."

"But our family," Greg pleaded, falling faster. "We talked about the children we wanted."

"My family is here." Although tears now filled her eyes, her face appeared at peace. "Ramón and all the other abused children who come here are my family. I can't leave them."

The pain sped to every single nerve in his being. Greg had hit bottom; he had lost Gwen.

She stood up, dismissing him. "Good-bye, Greg."

Anger and pain mixed to create a storm within him; it raged so violently that her face and the rest of the room blurred before him. He spun on his heels and fled.

"I will pray for you," she called after him. "I will pray that God grants you the same peace he's given me."

Greg ran out of the convent to his car. Tears streamed down his face, and he pounded the roof of his car until his knuckles were battered and bleeding. This was a merciful and loving God? He had so many women in the world from whom to choose his servants. Greg only had Gwen. God had taken his one and only love.

* * *

"Wow, that was a close one," the chauffeur called back to Victor as he fought the wheel to bring the large car under control. Victor gripped the arm rest in the back seat. Maybe he should have stayed in Chicago until the storm passed.

"Looks like the storm's getting worse," Victor told the driver. "You're welcome to stay the night if you want. I have a lot of spare rooms."

"Nah," the driver sneered as he stopped the car in front of Victor's house. "I haven't had so much fun since I was a kid. Once I get off that country road, it'll be smooth sailing. I'll slide all the way home."

"Suit yourself," Victor muttered. He stepped out and headed quickly toward the house. "Leave my luggage by the door," he shouted over his shoulder. "My houseman will get it."

As usual, Miguel had opened the door for him before he stepped up to it.

"Good evening, sir."

"Good evening." He handed Miguel his coat. Halfway up the stairs, Victor stopped and wrinkled his nose. The air was heavy with the scent of pine.

Suddenly something registered belatedly, sending alarms off in his brain. Miguel was just bringing the luggage in, and Victor rushed by him before the door was shut. Victor stood in a snowdrift as the wind wormed fingers of ice under his shirt. He stared at his house, which was lit up like a cheap bar.

"Damn," he shouted. Brightly colored lights winked at him through the snowflakes, and a bright star shone from atop the entryway. "Miguel," he screamed, "what the hell is going on here?"

His red-faced houseman stood in the entranceway, holding the door for him. Once Victor had come inside he closed the door and lingered uncomfortably at the foot of the stairs as Victor looked wildly about the foyer. More lights, evergreen garlands, ribbons . . .

"Miguel," he screamed again.

Miguel swallowed hard. "Sir, ah . . . ah we thought—"

Victor was furious. "You thought? I don't pay you to think. I pay you to keep this house in order."

Miguel's expression changed from discomfort to acute pain. "Miss Reed instructed us to—"

"Nikki?" Victor's eyes narrowed to slits. "Making my house look like a department store was her idea?"

Miguel's mouth opened, but no words came out.

"Where is she?"

The houseman pointed toward the living room.

Victor took a deep breath and swallowed his fury, then let his breath out slowly. When the spots in front of his eyes were eradicated, Victor slowly walked to the living room.

"Merry Christmas, Victor."

Victor first noticed the huge Norway spruce that thoroughly dominated his living room. Nikki was sitting in the conversation pit, feet up on the furniture, dressed in a short blue party dress. Her blond hair was fashioned in an almost tasteful set of curls.

He felt his blood pressure going up again. "What the hell is going on here?" he hissed.

"I wanted to give you the Christmas that you never had." Her voice was soft and tender. Nikki's whole appearance was different, and this transformation bothered him as much as the change she had wrought in his house.

"Never had? How do you know what I had or didn't have?"

His hands started shaking as she sent him a knowing smile. Fear mingled with Victor's rage, creating an explosive combination.

"How do you know what I had? Tell me."

Nikki blinked rapidly and sank back into the cushion, apparently feeling the heat of his rage.

"It's nothing to be ashamed of," she said. "A lot of people had rough childhoods. I should know."

"You pried," he shouted. "You stuck your damn nose where it didn't belong."

"I wanted to know you."

"Know me?" His voice slipped into a menacingwhisper. "Why do you need to know me?"

"Because you've done so much for me, Victor. I wanted to pay you back for all the good things you've given me. You've taught me to talk right, walk right, dress right, and—"

"I didn't do a damn thing for you."

He was back to screaming. Nikki stared in bewilderment.

"I did it because it was interesting. I was playing at Pygmalion."

"Pig what?"

"Pygma—" He waved his hands in disgust. "Forget it," he said. "You're too ignorant to understand."

Her face started crumbling around the edges, and she seemed to be on the verge of tears, but he didn't care. He went on shouting. "I just wanted to see if I could take a guttersnipe like you and turn you into something human. It was a challenge, a game, nothing more."

Slowly the soft edges of Nikki's soul turned hard, and her eyes became dry and clear.

Yet her reaction infuriated Victor even more, and he was seized with an insane desire to bat her down, to show her that he was more powerful than she would ever be, that she would never control him—*never!*

"And I nearly succeeded," he sneered. "The casual observer would have a hard time distinguishing you from a real lady."

"Congratulations, Victor."

The obvious contempt in the curl of her lips snapped Victor's last string. He flew into a rage, smashing the figures in the manger scene, ripping decorations off the tree and throwing them to the floor.

"What the hell is a common stripper like you trying to prove anyway?"

For a moment, a savage satisfaction warmed his heart as she burst into tears, turned, and ran from the room. Victor remained alone, breathing hard, until the fires of rage burned lower and lower within him.

Then remorse started nagging at him. She'd only been trying to please him, to give him what she thought he wanted. He went after her, but instead found Miguel, standing in the foyer staring at the open door and the snow piling up on the floor.

"What in the world is the matter with you?" Victor snapped. "Why are you letting the snow come in?"

"Miss Reed is gone, sir."

"What?"

"Miss Reed, sir. She's run out into the storm. Her coat is still here."

Worry edged into Victor's mind, pushing aside the welter of other emotions. Nikki was wandering in the raging storm. He remembered the bare-backed party dress she wore and the sling-back sandals. His anger fled, panic rushing in to take its place.

"Miguel, call the stable. Have them saddle Luther for me."

He felt sick, and his stomach twisted in pain. Why did he always turn against any woman who loved him? He stared out the open door. The soft flakes were turning into vicious little shards of ice, ice that could freeze and kill delicate beauty just as his words had killed Nikki's love. What had he done? Wasn't it enough that he had to drive her away from him? Had he had to drive her out into this blizzard, too? He would find her—before he had a dead woman on his hands—and he would set her straight once and for all. No one tampered with Victor Newman's life. The sooner Nikki learned that lesson, the better off she would be.

Soaps & Serials® Fans!

★ Order the *Soaps & Serials*® books you have missed in this series.

★ Collect other *Soaps & Serials*® series from their very beginnings.

★ Give *Soaps & Serials*® series as gifts to other fans.

...see other side for ordering information

You can now order previous titles
of *Soaps & Serials*® Books by Mail!

Just complete the order form, detach, and send together
with your check or money order payable to:

Soaps & Serials®
120 Brighton Road, Box 5201, Clifton, NJ 07015-5201

Please circle the book #'s you wish to order:

(A) The Young and The Restless	1 2 3 4 5 6 7 8 9 10 11 12 13 14
(B) Days of Our Lives	1 2 3 4 5 6 7 8 9 10 11 12 13 14
(C) Guiding Light	1 2 3 4 5 6 7 8 9 10 11 12 13 14
(D) Another World	1 2 3 4 5 6 7 8 9 10 11 12 13 14
(E) As The World Turns	1 2 3 4 5 6 7 8 9 10 11 12 13 14
(F) Dallas™	1 2 3 4 5 6 7 8 9 10 11 12 13 14
(G) Knots Landing™	1 2 3 4 5 6 7 8 9 10 11 12 13 14

Each book is $2.50 ($3.50 in Canada).
Total number of books
circled_____ × price above = $ _____

Sales tax (CT and NY residents only) $ _____

Shipping and Handling $ _____ .95

Total payment enclosed $ _____
(check or money orders only)

Name_____

Address _____ Apt# _____

City _____ State _____ Zip _____

Telephone (_____)
AREA CODE

COLUMBIA PICTURES
presents
YOUNG AND RESTLESS
Official Licensed Merchandise

For **FREE** brochure of all merchandise, send a self addressed, stamped, LEGAL size envelope to:

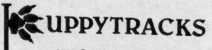UPPYTRACKS

6513 Lankershim Blvd.
No. Hollywood, California 91606